THE LOVES OF LORD GRANTON

Also by Marion Chesney in Large Print:

The Deception
The Intrigue
The Sins of Lady Dacey
Colonel Sandhurst to the Rescue
Sir Philip's Folly
Mrs. Budley Falls From Grace
Miss Tonks Turns to Crime
Lady Fortescue Steps Out
Yvonne Goes to York
Deborah Goes to Dover
Penelope Goes to Portsmouth
Emily Goes to Exeter
Marrying Harriet
Finessing Clarissa
Lucy

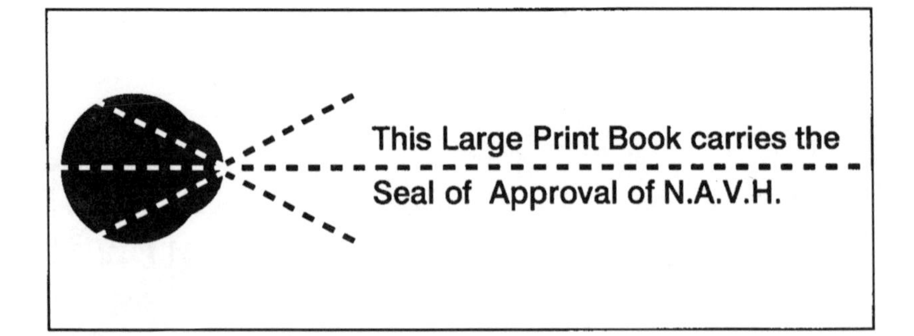

THE LOVES OF LORD GRANTON

Marion Chesney

G.K. Hall & Co.
Thorndike, Maine

Published in 1997 by arrangement with
Fawcett Books, a division of Random House, Inc.

G.K. Hall Large Print Romance Collection.

The text of this Large Print edition is unabridged.
Other aspects of the book may vary from the original edition.

Set in 16 pt. Plantin by Rick Gundberg.

Printed in the United States on permanent paper.

Library of Congress Cataloging in Publication Data

Chesney, Marion.
The loves of Lord Granton / Marion Chesney.
p. cm. — (Regency romance)
ISBN 0-7838-8301-3 (lg. print : hc : alk. paper)
1. Large type books. I. Title. II. Series.
[PR6053.H4535L68 1997]
823′.914—DC21 97-30533

For Annette Clayton, with best regards

Chapter One

Barton Sub Edge was a sleepy Cotswold village. Not much happened there and nobody supposed it ever would. The year of eighteen hundred and twelve saw an exceptionally fine summer, and the village seemed even sleepier than ever as it basked in long days of lazy sunlight where people moved languidly, thick roses clustered round cottage doors, and the thatched roofs of the houses shone like gold.

Tranquillity outside, however, does not mean tranquillity within, and such was the case in the rectory. The rector of Saint Peter and Saint Paul, Dr. Peter Hadley, had four grown-up daughters. The rector considered four unmarried daughters one of the many crosses the good Lord had given him to bear to test his faith. The fact that he had caused some of his burdens by marrying a silly, pretty lady with neither brains nor money to commend her never crossed his mind.

He should have been grateful that Mary, the eldest at twenty-one, considered herself the mainstay of the family and prided herself on her intelligence. But Mary had a way of giving little martyred sighs when asked to help about the parish, and self-appointed saints are always difficult to live with. Amy, at twenty, was pretty, frivolous, and as empty-headed as her mother. So, too, was the next in line, Harriet, aged nineteen. Then came Frederica, just turned eighteen, shy and damned as "difficult" because of her fey appearance and odd ways.

Mary, Amy, and Harriet felt that the long days of sunshine were intensifying the fact that they had little social life and no beaux. Frederica often wondered if it might be possible to die of boredom.

The social life of the village, such as it was, was dominated by "the great house," Townley Hall, home of baronet, Sir Giles Crown, and his lady. The rector was often invited to dinner, but his family only on general occasions such as balls and fetes to which the rest of the village came.

Mary Hadley had received a proposal of marriage when she was just nineteen. Her suitor was a local gentleman farmer, but at that time Mary had had her eye on the squire's son, Jeremy. Jeremy had been inconsiderate enough to join a regiment and take himself off the day after Mary had turned down the farmer, and the farmer had subsequently married little Jenny Pascoe, daughter of a Moreton-in-Marsh solicitor, and was now to all accounts blissfully happy. Only Mary thought she detected looks of lost love in his eyes when they occasionally met. Frederica thought it was wishful thinking on her sister's part. Mary was handsome in a severe way, with a pouter pigeon figure, a rather sallow skin, and a commanding air. She played the pianoforte and the harp, both competently, and wrote poetry that she read aloud whenever she had a captive audience.

One day when her sisters were fretting and quarreling, Frederica put on her bonnet and set out for a walk. The sun struck down on her back through the thin muslin of her gown, and she was glad when she reached the road out of the village where the tall hedges met above her head, sheltering her from the sun.

The girls had been educated at the local school, and Frederica had furthered her education by reading voraciously. She worried often about what her life was going to be. She wished with all her heart that she had been born a boy. She could have joined a regiment like the squire's son, or she could have read for the bar, or she could have done any number of things denied to women. All she could think of doing when she grew old enough to be considered respectable was to advertise for a post of governess and so escape the stifling hot grave that Barton Sub Edge seemed to be on that fine day.

Often her own boredom and discontent made her feel guilty. It seemed not so long ago that she had relished the beauty of the countryside and the changing seasons.

She came out of the shadow of the tall hedges and into the sunshine once more, climbed over a stile beside the road, and headed round the edge of a field of wheat toward Cummin Woods, which lay on the far side.

She paused once she was among the trees. A breeze far overhead ruffled the leaves. In the center of the wood lay a round dark pool, calm and secretive. Frederica stood by the pool and looked down at her reflection in the water. A thin face with large eyes and fine silvery hair under her sunbonnet looked up at her until a puff of wind ruffled the water and broke up her reflection.

She sat down with a little sigh. God, she thought dismally, had not blessed her with a feminine mind. For all their discontent, her sisters could easily become immersed in trivia, the latest bit of gossip, the latest fashion, or the social column in the newspaper, which was a week old by the time it was passed down to them from Townley Hall. In most other parts of the country, she would not be allowed to wander about unescorted, but Barton Sub Edge and the surrounding placid countryside had never been plagued with footpads or highwaymen.

Unlike her sisters, she never dreamed of beaux or romance. It had been dinned into her that her looks were "unfortunate," and she knew she was expected to spend the rest of her days at the rectory, after her prettier sisters were married, to be a companion to her mother.

She had no friends. Her mother was sharply aware of the social pecking order. Annabelle, Sir Giles Crown's beautiful daughter, would have been rated a suitable companion, but Annabelle was too high in the instep to befriend anyone from the rectory. The squire had only one son and no daughters. Everyone else was considered not socially high enough. She had made friends at school, but after her school days were over, it was borne in on her that such friendships were not suitable and must end, and Frederica had been brought up to believe that daughterly duty and obedience were next to godliness.

And, as she looked at the water, she had a sudden feeling that her life was to change, that something momentous was about to happen. Despite the heat, she gave a little shiver. Anxious to hold on to this feeling, although she was sure it was all in her imagination and that she would emerge from this wood and go back along the dusty road to home to find everything exactly as it had been, she began to hurry home with a mounting feeling of excitement.

With a little sigh, she made her way out of the wood. She held her skirts up as she walked around the edge of the wheat field. She was always being lectured on the state of her clothes.

Then as she reached the road and climbed the stile, she was aware of a damp feel to the breeze against her cheek and looked over to the west. Black clouds were mounting up against the sky. A storm was coming. She rushed along the road. By the time she reached the end of it and came out by the wall of the churchyard, the sky above was black and she heard the first growl of thunder.

She walked into the churchyard and round the

square Norman building of the church to the rectory on the far side.

The first thing she heard when she entered was the babble of excited voices from the rectory parlor.

She walked in. Her mother and sisters broke off their conversation on seeing her, and Mrs. Hadley let out a little shriek. "Just look at you, Frederica! Dusty, like the veriest peasant. What will Lord Granton think!"

"Who," demanded Frederica, "is Lord Granton?"

Viscount, Lord Rupert Granton, sat in the bay window of White's and stared gloomily out at the sun blazing down on Saint James's.

"Did you say Barton Sub Edge?" queried his friend, Major Harry Delisle. "Where in creation is that?"

"It is a village in the Cotswolds. I have accepted an invitation from Sir Giles Crown to stay, and so I engineered an invitation for you as well."

"Why?"

"Because I am bored out of my wits and regret having decided to go to this forgotten hamlet in the middle of nowhere and decided you should suffer as well."

"I say," protested the major, a round, chubby, shortsighted man sweltering in all the latest fashion of starched cravat, starched shirt points, and skintight pantaloons.

"Well, we are frying here in the poisonous and disease-ridden heat of a London summer. Everyone has gone to their estates or followed the Prince Regent to Brighton. I am of a mind to get married, and Annabelle Crown is described as a beauty."

"When did you meet her?"

"I didn't. Just heard about her."

"So why have you decided to get married all of a sudden?"

"I have been racketing around all my life and am still bored. Marriage is the one diversion I have not tried."

"Seasons come and Seasons go, and you have had ample opportunity to find a bride," pointed out his friend.

"But I never thought of marriage until now," said the viscount, stifling a yawn.

Viscount Granton had been described as looking like the devil himself. He had thick black hair that grew in a widow's peak on his forehead, glittering amber eyes that could blaze yellow when he was angry, a proud nose, and a firm but sensuous mouth in a tanned face. His figure was as lithe and muscular as that of an acrobat. His reputation as a rake did not stop his still being regarded as a marital prize.

"And what will you do when you are married?" asked the major cynically. "Leave your lady in the country and go back to rattling about Town?"

"I am weary of rattling. I am searching for something, and I do not know what that something is. I would like sons and perhaps to spend more time on my estates."

"You have an excellent agent."

"Do I? I suppose I do. Parton keeps saying, 'Everything is running smoothly, my lord. No need for you to trouble about anything.' I mention the latest advances in agriculture and ask him if he has tried the new phosphates, and he smiles and says, 'You must not trouble yourself, my lord. Everything is as it should be,' and I am left feeling like some dilettante aristocrat who wishes to play like Marie Antoinette. You're bored, too, aren't you?"

"I'm always bored out of Season and away from my regiment. I thought this long leave would be fun, but I confess to feeling jaded."

"Then there you have it." The viscount stifled another yawn. "We may as well go to this remote village and be jaded and bored together."

"But I do not understand," protested Frederica, raising her voice so that she could be heard above the tumult of the storm that was now raging overhead. "Why all the excitement? Sir Giles, it appears, is hopeful that this Lord Granton will propose marriage to his Annabelle, who is rich and beautiful. Why would such a man decide to favor one of the daughters of the rectory?"

"You see," said Mary, her voice shrill with excitement, "Annabelle may be beautiful and rich, but she did not take at the last Season because she is very dull. Worldly men such as this Lord Granton prefer women of brains and character. I shall read him some of my poems."

"Stoopid," said Amy with a toss of auburn curls and a contemptuous flash of her blue eyes, "gentlemen do not like clever women; everyone knows that."

"Exactly," agreed black-haired Harriet. "You would prose him to death, Mary."

"We shall see," said Mary complacently. "May I remind you that I am the only one who has received a proposal of marriage."

"Never mind all that," said Amy. "Frederica, you must help me make over my ball gown. Lady Giles has sent us a fashion magazine, and the neck of my gown is too high."

"And I must collect my portfolio of watercolors and see that they are all there!" exclaimed Harriet. "He will want to see those."

"How old is Lord Granton?" asked Frederica.

"Early thirties."

"And not wed! Why is that?"

"Oh, he has such a *wicked* reputation!" cried Amy, clapping her hands. "He is nicknamed Devil Granton. It is said a lady once tried to commit suicide because he had broken her heart. He has fought duels. He has traveled abroad. He is supposed to be a dangerous man."

Frederica began to look amused. She turned to her mother. "You are surely not hoping that this wicked man should turn out to be attracted to one of your daughters?"

"All men are wicked," said Mrs. Hadley. She was a plump little woman with large blue eyes. "They always reform after marriage."

"Is that what happened to Papa?"

"Frederica, behave yourself. That sarcastic levity you sometimes betray is not at all the thing. Quite unladylike, in fact. Oh, do go and change your gown. What if Lord Granton should arrive early and decide to call at the rectory?"

"In the middle of a storm, Mama?"

"Go to your room, *now*. It is as well that we have no hopes of a marriage for *you*."

Frederica made her way up the stairs. The thunder was now grumbling away in the distance. She opened the window and leaned out with her elbows on the sill. The air was sweet and fresh, full of the scent of flowers and trees. A shaft of sun shone down from behind a black cloud, and all the raindrops hanging from the flowers and bushes in the rectory garden glittered gold.

A little spark of rebellion burned somewhere deep inside Frederica. She was tired of being damned as plain and unmarriageable. She went back into the room and sat down in front of the toilet table and removed her bonnet. Her silvery blond hair was worn straight down her back. Frederica was of an age to have her hair put up, but with three unmarried elder sisters, she was still considered the baby of the family. She twisted her hair up on top of her head and looked at herself consideringly. Her eyes were large and gray. Her skin was good and her lips well shaped.

But she was too slim in an age when the full figure was fashionable; her face was too thin when ladies still plumped out their cheeks with wax pads.

She gave a little sigh. The strange excitement she had felt at the pool must have been because of the approaching storm. The imminent arrival of a rake in their sleepy village would not alter her life one whit.

Sir Giles Crown was a portly man, always conscious of his standing in the neighborhood. He and his wife had accompanied their daughter, of course, to the last Season in London. Sir Giles had not enjoyed London one bit. In the countryside he was a big fish in a small pool, but in London he had been considered a very minor luminary. Annabelle's beauty, too, had been somewhat eclipsed by an unexpected number of fine-looking debutantes at the Season. That, Sir Giles and his lady had decided, must have been the reason for Annabelle's strange failure to secure a husband. He had written to Lord Granton, although he had only had a fleeting club acquaintanceship with the younger man, and was now proud and pleased that his invitation had been accepted.

His wife, thin and fussy, with cold pale eyes and narrow lips that always seemed to be primped up in disapproval, was planning entertainments for the distinguished guest.

"We shall have a ball," she said, "but we must

make sure it is an elegant affair. Lord Granton would not appreciate a room full of villagers."

"I suppose those silly girls from the rectory will be angling for invitations," said Annabelle. Annabelle Crown had glossy dark brown hair and large liquid brown eyes. Her mouth was small enough to please the highest stickler and she had a well-turned ankle. But she carried with her an air of cold haughtiness she had learned from her mother. She, too, had hated London, where no one seemed to be impressed by her whatsoever. She had never been in the way of making friends, and so had felt excluded from the gossip and chatter of the other debutantes. She had been relieved and excited to learn of this Lord Granton's forthcoming visit, which she firmly believed was tantamount to a proposal of marriage, although he had never danced with her once during the Season. She assumed he had seen her and been struck by her beauty but was initially too conscious of his rakish reputation to make any approach.

"Such as Lord Granton," said her mother, "is not going to be at all interested in any of the girls from the rectory. Only think what he would make of Mary Hadley, prosing on with her dreadful poems, not to mention the vulgar giggling and ogling and whispering of Harriet and Amy, and Frederica is too young and strange to merit a second glance. I think we may be assured that you have no competition in the county whatsoever, Annabelle."

"I suppose you have the right of it, Mama," said Annabelle.

"And he will be *here*," said her mother. "You will take walks together and dine together. Nothing can spoil your chances."

"He does have a wild reputation, Mama."

"That was in his youth. All men are wild before marriage."

A rare gleam of amusement lit up Annabelle's brown eyes. "Was Papa wild before his marriage?"

"Alas, yes, my dear," said Sir Giles, ruefully shaking his head. "But once I met your mama, I became a reformed character." Sir Giles was fond of referring to his hellfire youth when in fact it had been staid and dull and deprived of either adventure or incident. He had inherited Townley Hall from his father and had lived there ever since.

It was a large, square, comfortable mansion bedecked with many bad oil paintings. Art, as Sir Giles was fond of saying, was his one weakness, but he had an unfailing eye for the tasteless and mediocre and liked to brag of discovering hitherto unknown artists, which meant their services had not cost much. Witness to this was a family portrait of himself, his wife, and his daughter that hung in the drawing room which showed them grouped round a pedestaled urn in the gardens of the Hall. Sir Giles was leaning on the urn, his legs nonchalantly crossed. The artist had not been very good at legs. Lady Giles stared out of the canvas with a peculiar expression of outrage on her face, and her daughter, seated on the very green grass at her feet, looked as if she was about to be sick. The artist had meant to portray a dove flying overhead, but it appeared to be growing out of the top of Lady Crown's hat.

They maintained a large staff of servants who were loyal to them, jobs being hard to find in the country.

"Where are you going?" Lady Crown asked her husband as he rose to his feet and began to pull on his gloves.

"I am going to call on Hadley at the rectory," said Sir Giles. "I have some parish matters to discuss with him."

"I will come with you," said Annabelle, who suddenly craved an audience for her "triumph."

Soon they were entering the rectory drawing room to be pleasantly fussed and fawned over by Mrs. Hadley.

"Do tell us all about this Lord Granton," begged Amy, while Harriet chorused, "Yes, do tell."

Annabelle gave a satisfied little smile. "I really do not think I should discuss my fiancé with you."

Frederica was not present. Mary, Amy, and Harriet looked at Annabelle in dismay. "We did not know you were to be wed!" exclaimed Mary, thinking of the poem she had started working on to impress Lord Granton.

"My daughter is joking," Sir Giles said hurriedly. "Lord Granton is simply coming on a visit."

"Then why did you call him your fiancé?" demanded Mary.

Annabelle adopted what she hoped was a worldly air. "When an unmarried gentleman travels to the country to stay at the home of a friend who has an unmarried daughter, then it is a foregone conclusion that he has marriage in mind."

"But he has not actually proposed," insisted Mary.

"Oh, I am sure he will," said Annabelle, smoothing down a fold of her skirt.

She noticed to her annoyance that the girls had visibly brightened again, and resolved to make sure that Lord Granton never called at the rectory. Sir Giles was now deep in conversation with the rector.

The door opened and Frederica came in. She curtsied to Sir Giles — who did not notice her — and then to Annabelle.

"We are trying to find out all about Lord Granton, Frederica," said Amy.

"I thought we already knew all there was to know." Frederica sat down with that vague air of boredom that always seemed to cling to her. Annabelle surveyed her with irritation.

"And what could such as *you* know about the viscount?" demanded Annabelle.

"Gossip," replied Frederica, turning to look through the window at a blackbird pecking for worms on the lawn. "That Lord Granton is a heartbreaking rake who nearly drove one lady to suicide and who has fought a duel."

"I do not like to think that our guest is being gossiped about in this vulgar way." Annabelle bridled. "How did you come by such tittle-tattle?"

Mrs. Hadley shot a fulminating look at Frederica and rushed into the breach. "You must realize, Miss Annabelle, that we at our humble rectory always have your welfare at heart." Poor Mrs. Hadley saw any hopes of invitations to social events fading away. She began to praise Annabelle fulsomely on her gown and her beauty until Annabelle began to smile. Mrs. Hadley had in fact culled the gossip from one of her own maids who was friend to a maid at the Hall who had eavesdropped on her employers.

Lord Granton and Major Delisle arrived at Townley Hall a week later under a blistering sun on an exceedingly humid day.

As his carriage bowled up the long drive to the Hall Lord Granton experienced an unusual frisson of excitement. He felt suddenly sure that something exciting was going to enter his life. This Miss Annabelle Crown had been at the Season, that much he had learned from her father, but he could not quite bring her face to mind. Perhaps for once in his dissolute life, he might actually fall in love.

He and Delisle climbed down from the carriage. Sir Giles himself came out to meet them.

"Welcome!" he cried. "You are both welcome. Come in, come in! You must be tired after your long journey."

He would have taken both of them to the drawing room to introduce them to his wife and daughter, but Lord Granton protested that he would like to bathe and change out of his traveling clothes. So the butler took them abovestairs and showed them two well-appointed bedchambers. Lord Granton's valet set about laying out clean clothes for his master and demanded that a bath be carried up.

Downstairs in the drawing room, Annabelle and her mother waited impatiently.

But Lord Granton, after he had bathed, realized he had not had much sleep the night before, and the heaviness and heat of the day were making his eyes droop.

He climbed into the high bed and fell soundly asleep and was awakened much later by the ringing of the dressing bell.

His valet appeared and said, "The family dine at six, my lord."

Not quite country hours but not London either, thought Lord Granton, stretching and yawning. Major Harry Delisle came in and lounged in a chair by the window while Lord Granton was dressed. He looked out the window.

"Pleasant here," he said, "after the hurly and burly of London."

"There wasn't much hurly-burly when we were there," pointed out Lord Granton, his voice muffled by the cambric shirt his valet was pulling over his head. "Everyone had left Town." His head emerged. "I trust our hostess is not offended by our nonappearance, but I confess I was deuced tired."

"Guilty of the same thing," said the major. "Slept like a log."

He waited patiently while the viscount was helped into a black evening coat, knee breeches, silk clocked stockings, and pumps. "I wonder what Miss Annabelle is like," commented the major, watching the viscount's long white fingers searching in his jewel box for a stick pin.

"We shall see." Lord Granton deftly placed a sapphire in the snowy folds of his cravat. "Let us join the ladies."

When they entered the drawing room, various people rose to greet him. He bowed to Lady Giles and turned and bowed to Annabelle, his eyes registering appreciatively that the girl was indeed pretty. She was wearing a white silk gown with an overdress of green silk, and on her head was one of the new Turkish turbans. She dimpled and curtsied prettily.

Then he and the major were introduced to the rest of the company, Squire Huxtable and his wife, a Lord and Lady Blackstone, and the rector, Dr. Hadley.

The conversation at dinner Lord Granton damned as dull and provincial. But his friend, Harry Delisle, was not so critical. He appeared enchanted by Annabelle and happy with the company. The dinner was excellent and the wine good. Warm evening air floated in through the open windows. The major began to feel happy and relaxed. The viscount found the company boring: Harry found it undemanding and pleasant.

Why cannot I relax and appreciate this company, this life? wondered Lord Granton. Why am I so critical? I found London increasingly tedious. Miss Annabelle is vastly taking. It is bad mannered and ungrateful of me to show my boredom.

He set himself to please, telling anecdotes of London life that the company eagerly absorbed and saved up for subsequent less distinguished dinner parties.

When the ladies retired and the port was passed around, Lord Granton addressed the rector. "It is a difficult life in the country for a parson, I think, when you have no wife to support you in the parish duties."

"On the contrary, my lord," said Dr. Hadley, looking puzzled. "I do have a wife and four daughters."

"They are not indisposed, I trust?"

"No, my lord, all are well."

Lord Granton raised his thin brows. He had never approved of the practice of clergymen being invited to dinner at great houses while their wives and families were excluded. He thought that in Dr. Hadley's place he would have refused the invitation and then immediately realized that Dr. Hadley could not do so because he owed his living to the Crowns.

"So you have four daughters," he pursued. "A heavy liability."

"I would have liked a son," said Mr. Hadley ruefully. "What man would not? And yet my girls are good and beautiful. Mary, the eldest, is very clever and talented; Amy and Harriet are pretty and charming."

"You said four daughters."

"Ah, yes, there is also Frederica." He fell silent.

"Tell me about Frederica," inquired Lord Granton curiously.

"There is nothing much to tell, my lord. I am very fond of my youngest. Frederica is but eighteen years, and alas, what can a young girl expect in life but a suitable marriage? Frederica, unlike her sisters, is a trifle plain and too bookish."

"Ah, novels."

"Not entirely. Works of travel, Greek classics, philosophy — most unfeminine."

"I am of the opinion that a young lady with a well-informed mind would have well-informed children."

"Provided she did not have girls," said Dr. Hadley with an indulgent laugh. "Sir Giles, this is most excellent port. I am always saying that the fare in the Hall rivals that of the best London tables."

Lord Granton took a mild dislike to the rector. He surely did not need to *fawn* so blatantly. He wondered about this Frederica. If the little girl was bookish, it followed that she was intelligent and sensitive. How did she view her father's behavior in front of the Crowns? He dismissed the question. Toad-eating was the way of the world.

Annabelle played the harp for them when they joined the ladies in the drawing room. Her plump white arms moved smoothly over the strings. The light from an oil lamp behind her shone on her face. Outside the long open French windows, birds chirped sleepily in the branches to the sound of the harp.

Perhaps I have been looking for contentment in the wrong places, thought Lord Granton. Perhaps I should retire to the country and forget London and foreign parts.

At the end of the evening, Sir Giles said the family would be going to church in the morning, the following day being a Sunday. Perhaps Lord Granton would like to rest instead?

But the viscount said he would be delighted to attend. Annabelle thought of making an entrance in the church with him and wondered if she could somehow get him to take her arm.

When they entered the gloom of the church the following morning, Annabelle was accompanied by her mother while the gentlemen walked behind.

The Hadley girls were already in their pew,

one of the high old-fashioned type that blocked off a view of anything much other than the altar and the pulpit.

Dr. Hadley preached a surprisingly good sermon. Amy and Harriet fidgeted and giggled and whispered all through it. Amy longed to stand up and look over the back of the pew to see if Lord Granton was in the church. Mary frowned at her two livelier sisters. She was sure Lord Granton had only to see *her* to be struck by the fineness of her eyes. The Hadley sisters were in their best gowns with the exception of Frederica, who was wearing a simple white muslin and a wide-brimmed straw hat decorated with a wreath of daisies plucked from the rectory lawn. Mrs. Hadley noticed those "ridiculous" daisies only when they all rose at the end of the service to leave the pew, but she scarcely could snatch the offending flowers from her daughter's bonnet in the middle of the church.

Annabelle had told her mother to make sure the Hadley girls were not introduced to either Lord Granton or his friend Major Delisle "for they will push themselves forward so, Mama."

But it was the major who noticed the girls clustered behind their father on the church porch. "Do introduce us to your family, Rector," he said.

Lord Granton noticed the rolling-eyed look of a frightened horse that the rector cast in the direction of Lady Crown. But the man dutifully did introduce his wife, then Mary, Amy, and

Harriet. The major wondered if Mary suffered from indigestion because on curtsying to himself and Lord Granton, she primped up her lips and fixed Granton with a steady look and winced. Mary was trying to convey to Lord Granton that she was his intellectual equal and not like Amy and Harriet, who were giggling and flirting with their eyes over their fans.

"Four daughters," said Lord Granton. "That's what you said, Dr. Hadley. Where is the fourth?"

"Oh, Frederica," said the rector dismally. "She is somewhere about."

"Frederica!" called Mrs. Hadley shrilly. "Come here!"

Lord Granton looked over their heads and saw a slim figure approaching them through the tombstones. Frederica was wearing a muslin gown that hung rather loosely on her slim body. He wondered if it was one of her plumper sisters' hand-me-downs. On her head was a shady straw bonnet embellished with daisies around the crown. Her silvery fair hair was worn straight down her back, and as she came nearer, he could see that her large gray eyes held a wary look.

Lord Granton felt bored and restless again. What on earth was he doing standing in a country churchyard, striving to be pleasant to dull people? Frederica was introduced to him. He met her gaze and received a slight jolt. For in those large eyes boredom such as he himself was enduring was plain to see.

"How delightful to make your acquaintance,

Miss Frederica," he said.

She did not reply, merely nodding slightly and looking gravely at him.

"The weather is very fine, is it not?" he pursued.

But her three sisters pushed forward, answering for her, assuring this handsome lord that, yes, the weather was tremendously fine, that they thought the thunderstorm had marked the end of the good weather, but wonder upon wonders, the sun had shone again; he must have brought the good weather with him. And all the while the banter and flirting went on, his eyes followed Frederica, who was once more moving away.

He was amazed that Frederica's lack of interest in him should cause him pique. He continued to watch her until she had rounded the corner of the church and disappeared from view.

Chapter Two

Had Major Delisle been as bored as his friend, Lord Granton would have found some excuse to take his leave. However, the major kept saying how jolly country life was and what a splendid time they were having and how pretty Miss Annabelle was, and the viscount did not have the heart to spoil his fun.

They went on picnics and rides through the heavy Cotswold air and under a burning remorseless sun.

Annabelle flirted and chattered prettily, but the more she flirted and the more she chattered, the lower Lord Granton's spirits fell.

One afternoon after he had endured a week at Townley Hall and after a particularly filling dinner, he pleaded a headache and slipped out of the hall after changing into top boots and breeches. He made his way down the long drive under the fluttering lime trees and headed briskly along the road, feeling more relaxed and free as he put distance between himself and his hosts.

He saw a small wood off to his right and climbed over a stile and around a field and entered the wood, enjoying the late sunlight slanting through the trees. At the end of a winding path, he saw the dark gleam of water. He came out at a still, round pool and there, sitting on a mossy bank at the edge of it, he found Frederica. She had her back to him, but she was hatless and he recognized that odd silvery hair.

He wanted the evening to himself and turned around to retreat, but his boot cracked on a dried twig. He knew she would hear it, so he reluctantly turned back. Frederica rose to her feet and curtsied. She looked poised for flight.

"I am sorry I disturbed your meditations," he said.

"I was about to leave, my lord."

It was the first time he had heard her voice. It was calm and clear. He surprised himself by saying, "Stay with me a little. This is a pretty spot and the cool of the evening is welcome."

"But we are not chaperoned, my lord."

"Neither we are. But who is to know? And despite my wicked reputation, I am not about to attack you."

Frederica suddenly smiled, a bewitching smile. "Are you really so bad, my lord?"

"Let us sit down and I will try to redeem my character."

Frederica obediently sat down again, and he lowered himself onto the mossy knoll beside her.

"My bad reputation is based on the exploits of my youth."

"Are you so old?"

"I am thirty-one years. You, I believe, are eighteen. I must seem very old to you."

Frederica gave a little sigh. "Everyone seems very old to me."

"Explain."

"I think it is because I do not quite fit in anywhere, as if I am standing at the door to a ball to which I have not been invited."

"So how do you pass your days in this strange and alien world?"

"I read a great deal; I go for walks. This is my favorite place. There is peace here."

"But do you not help your mother and father with parish work?"

"Oh, yes, I sew for the poor and visit the sick, things like that. I think I must have a vulgar soul. I sometimes feel more at ease with the common villagers than with my own class, although being a rector's daughter is rather like being neither fish nor fowl — too grand for the villagers and not grand enough for Townley Hall."

"Are you usually so frank?"

"No, but the circumstance is unusual. Do tell me about your wicked youth. You fought a duel, did you not?"

"Yes."

"Over a lady."

"That was the case."

"Tell me about it. Was the lady divinely fair?"

He looked at her, half in exasperation, half in amusement. "I do not want to sully your ears with my early amours. The lady was of the demimonde. Yes, she was quite beautiful."

"And you were madly in love?"

"No, my chuck, I have never been madly in love with anyone. It was a matter of honor."

Frederica looked at him doubtfully. "A lady of the demimonde whom you did not love? I do not see where honor enters into it."

"She was unfaithful to me."

"But that surely was her profession!"

"Not when she was in my keeping."

"So you fought a duel with your rival in Hyde Park."

"No, at Chalk Farm."

"Swords?"

"Pistols."

"Did you kill him?" asked Frederica in a low voice. A little breeze stirred her silvery hair and blew a strand of it across her face.

"I winged him, quite deliberately. Had I killed him, I would have had to flee the country."

"And so you returned triumphantly to the arms of your lady?"

"I returned, yes, but to give her her marching orders."

Frederica heaved a disappointed little sigh. "It is always thus. The stuff that is portrayed in novels always smacks of high romance, but in real life it is always low and sordid."

"You have a sharp tongue, miss! I do not like being called low and sordid."

"I am sorry." Frederica blushed. "I am not usually so tactless. Put it down to the unusual circumstances of our meeting. Tell me about the lady who tried to commit suicide over you."

"So that you may damn my antics as sordid?"

"It is a different world to anything I have known or am likely to know, my lord. I am living vicariously."

"Oh, very well. The lady was a widow of the ton. She was flirtatious, light, and happy — frivolous. She led me to believe she had no interest in marriage or, indeed, in respectability. Am I shocking you?"

"No, I have heard that ladies in London take lovers and nobody minds just so long as they are not found out."

"The liaison," he went on, "began to degenerate. She began to flirt with other men to make me jealous. Then she began to throw things. She threw a scent bottle at my head. It missed me and struck the door and sent a cascade of Miss In Her Teens all over me. I stank like a civet cat. I detached myself. She had no intention of committing suicide, only in staging a suicide. I was supposed to feel guilty and rush back to her."

"Which you did not?"

He shook his head.

"And after that? Did you take another mistress?"

"Miss Frederica! This conversation must end. You are a daughter of the rectory. Behave like one!"

"I am always being told to behave. Perhaps I had better go."

"Tell me about yourself."

"There is nothing to tell. I was brought up in

this village. I went to school in this village. When my sisters are married, I shall stay on in this village until I die."

"And why should you not get married?"

"I am not pretty."

"Not in the common way, not in the fashionable way. But you have a rare beauty."

She turned and looked full at him, her eyes shining. "Oh, my lord, if only I could believe you. That is the most wonderful thing anyone has ever said to me."

He felt a tug at his heart.

Then her face fell. "But, of course, you are in the way of paying compliments."

"I once was, but not anymore. If I praise a lady's looks, I really mean it."

"Thank you. I shall treasure your comments. Perhaps I shall not stay in the village all my life. I have a plan." Frederica hugged her knees and stared into the black waters of the pool like a fortune teller looking into a crystal. "Perhaps when I am older, I shall advertise for a position as a governess."

"That would be jumping out of the frying pan into the fire, Miss Frederica. You say you are neither fish nor fowl here, but it would be the same in a large household, not on a par with your employers and not quite belonging among the servants either."

"It is the boredom, you see," said Frederica in a low voice. "It is a malaise."

"I suffer from almost perpetual boredom myself, my sweeting, although not at this precise moment. Perhaps our boredom is caused by ingratitude."

"I do not understand."

"Take my situation, for example. I am titled, rich, and not ill-favored. Instead of being grateful for all this, I feel a weariness of the soul."

"Papa tells me I am not in a state of grace."

"Perhaps neither of us is."

Frederica suddenly jumped to her feet. "I must go."

"I would like to continue our conversation," he said, rising as well. "Shall I call at the rectory?"

"Oh, no, my lord, such a call would be misinterpreted, and I would be put into my best gown and made to show you my watercolors, which are indifferent. And Sir Giles would be so angry that Papa might lose his living."

She turned, poised for flight.

"At least let me accompany you as far as the rectory."

"That would not answer, my lord. I have my reputation to consider."

She curtsied and moved away from him.

"Stay! Meet me here, say, in three days' time."

Frederica hesitated. "I must ask you why."

"Despite the difference in our ages, I feel we could be friends."

That delightful smile of hers once more illumined her face.

"I should like that."

"I shall be here at the same time."

He stood and watched her as she flitted away through the trees, and with an amused shake of his head, he began to follow her out of the wood, keeping a discreet distance from her in case they should be seen together.

Frederica made her way around the back of the rectory and let herself in by a little-used door. Because the Elizabethan building with its many staircases and sloping passages had originally been built for a very large family, she had the luxury of her own room. It was at the top of a staircase, not even used by the servants, and so she was able to slip quietly into her room. She sat on her bed. She, Frederica Hadley, had found a friend!

Lord Granton made his way slowly to the Hall. What an unusual little girl Frederica Hadley was. She amused him, and he could not quite remember when anyone had last done that.

He managed to reach his room without meeting anyone. He crossed to the window and looked out at the calm evening. He would meet Frederica one more time and then perhaps he would persuade the major that they had stayed at Townley Hall long enough. He knew that Annabelle's parents hoped he would propose to their daughter.

He turned as the door behind him opened and Major Harry Delisle walked in. "How's the headache?" asked Harry.

"I didn't have one. I found the company tedious and went out for a walk."

"Nothing will ever please you, will it?" demanded Harry crossly. "Here we are in this beautiful spot and during one of the best summers I can ever remember and all you do is gloom about the place."

"I will endeavor to look more cheerful tomorrow. What have our hosts arranged for us?"

"We are to go to the Blackstones'. They have a ruin they want us to see."

"Everyone has a ruin. Do they have a hermit as well?"

"Not that I know of. Rupert, you might make a push to be civil to Miss Crown. She is a sweet girl, and she plays the harp divinely."

"My ideas of marriage have fled. What of you, Harry? If you want to propose to the Annabelle chit, you have my blessing."

"She won't look at me as long as you're around."

"Oh, she will soon tire of my lack of attention."

"Tell you something I've noticed," complained the major. "I've never ever seen you actually enjoy a conversation with any female."

"There is one who amuses me," said Lord Granton, half to himself.

"Who is she?"

"What? Oh, someone I once met."

The following day Lord Granton gloomily surveyed the ruin of an Elizabethan watch tower. "Is it not romantic?" Annabelle asked breathily.

"It's falling down," pointed out the viscount.

"But do you not imagine what it was like in olden days?" cried Annabelle. "Can you not imagine a fair lady at the top watching her knight riding toward her?"

"There would be no reason for any maiden to be up on that tower," retorted the viscount. "I see a few small, squat, burly archers with long bows."

She rapped him playfully with her fan. "You are not romantic." She turned toward Delisle. "Is he, Major?"

"Never was," said the major. "Now I see *you,* Miss Annabelle, at the top of that tower with your hair streaming down your back and a rose in your hand."

Annabelle looked at the chubby major as if seeing him for the first time. "Why, Major Delisle, you are a true romantic and your wicked friend is not!"

Lord Granton stifled a yawn. Why, on this scorching day, had he to endure wearing full morning dress of blue swallowtail coat, starched cravat, breeches, and Hessian boots? It was a day for lying in the cool grass under a tree and reading a good book.

The ruin was some distance across the Blackstone estate from the house, but Lord and Lady Blackstone were indefatigable walkers. Not only were they to admire the ruin at one boundary of the estate but a stream at the west boundary and a stand of ornamental trees at the east.

Lord Granton could feel his cravat wilting and his hair under his hat becoming damp with sweat.

His thoughts strayed to that cool wood and the pool where he had met Frederica. If Frederica had been of the company, he would have had someone to talk to. But then he could hardly talk about how boring he found everyone with his hosts listening. He wondered how long the visit was to last. They had not been asked to bring evening clothes, so he could hope for escape by the late afternoon.

"It is too bad," complained Amy over the tea tray at the rectory. "None of us has had a chance to charm this Lord Granton. Bessie tells me her friend Maggie at the Hall says he is very handsome but quite haughty and cold and shows no interest in Annabelle whatsoever. Papa, you must get him to call."

"You should not listen to servants' gossip," admonished Dr. Hadley. Bessie was their maid, and her friend, Maggie, was one of the maids at the Hall.

Harriet pouted. "How are we to know what goes on if we do not listen to servants' gossip? If Lord Granton is as bored as he is said to be, he will soon take himself off and we will never get to know him. Do you not want good marriages for your daughters?"

"A viscount is a trifle too high for the daughters

of the rectory," said Dr. Hadley.

"Oh, come now, Dr. Hadley," protested his wife. "Our girls have much more to offer than Annabelle Crown. Mary is more talented, and Amy and Harriet are far prettier."

"I cannot be seen to be putting myself forward."

"But surely," his wife responded, "you might see his lordship when you are on your rounds and ask him if he would like some refreshment?"

"Perhaps," said the rector. "But you have all, except Frederica, been wearing your best gowns since his arrival in the hope that he might call."

Frederica smiled. "If you would forget about Lord Granton and wear your oldest gowns, that is bound to encourage his arrival at our doorstep."

"What can you mean, you silly widgeon?" snapped Mary.

"It is rather like waiting for a kettle to boil," said Frederica vaguely. "If you stand around and wait for it to boil, it seems to take ages, but if you go away and do something else, it seems to boil quite quickly."

"Fool!" said Harriet. "I can just imagine your brand of conversation fascinating our handsome lord, Frederica."

Frederica dreamily helped herself to another cake. Her sisters' insults could no longer touch her. How furious they would be if they learned that not only had she talked to Lord Granton but he wanted to see her again.

Frederica found that the afternoon she was to meet him seemed ages away and the time dragged slowly along, and then as the time approached for her to slip out of the house, the minutes seemed to race by.

She wished she had a new gown to wear or at least a smart new bonnet. She sighed as she changed into a clean but worn muslin gown. It had been Amy's. She took out her pin box and pinned it in a little so that it would fit her slender figure better. She really must begin to pay more attention to her clothes. It was time she began to properly alter her sisters' gowns that had been handed down to her.

With a fast-beating heart, she crept down what she thought of as her secret staircase and made her way through the garden and then across the churchyard, threading her way between the old sloping tombstones, which cast long shadows on the grass under the setting sun.

On the road she heard the rumble of carriage wheels and drew back into the hedgerow. It was a local farmer going home with his wife. She waited until the cart was out of sight and then reemerged from the shelter of the hedge, fretfully plucking out twigs and leaves that had become caught in the fine muslin of her gown.

Walking around the edge of the field, she felt very exposed to view and prayed no one else would pass on the road and see her. With a feeling of relief, she walked into the cool shadow of the trees.

Somehow she had expected he would be waiting by the pool, but when she found the area deserted, she reminded herself severely that no exact time had been fixed and sat down to wait.

She waited and waited while the sun sank lower and lower. Then as long shadows stole through the woods, it was with dismay that she finally looked up through the trees and saw the first stars gleaming in the night sky.

Of course he would not come. How silly she had been! He probably thought of her, if he thought of her at all, as a pert little schoolgirl who had briefly amused him.

Lord Granton sat in the drawing room and fretted as Annabelle kept on playing the harp. He felt he could not rise abruptly and leave the room. Would she never finish? The Blackstones were visiting for the evening. Lord Blackstone had fallen asleep and was snoring gently. Sir Giles and Lady Crown beamed at their indefatigable daughter as she played on and on and kept flashing little looks at Lord Granton to see how he was enjoying the performance.

By the time Annabelle had finished and the tea tray was brought in and he was able to murmur excuses and make his escape to his room, he found, looking out of the window, that it was already dark outside. Poor little Frederica! She would probably be tucked up in bed by now. But he changed rapidly into clothes suitable for walking: a cambric shirt, a comfortable old coat, cotton breeches, and top boots. He hesitated. With the company still downstairs, there would be a lot of coming and going across the hall. Feeling like a guilty schoolboy, he opened his window wide. A stout creeper clung to the wall outside. With a grin, he swung himself over the windowsill and climbed nimbly down.

He did not expect to find her still at the pool, but he was determined to go anyway, and then he would visit the rectory and try to convey a message to her that he had kept his promise.

He walked into the dim hush of the wood, suddenly grateful for the peace and quiet of the night. And he saw a glimmer of white by the pool. She was still there!

"Frederica!" he called.

Frederica quickly masked the look of real gladness and relief on her face as she slowly rose and turned around.

"I thought you had forgotten, my lord."

"Not I. Annabelle was playing that damned harp of hers forever. I could hardly walk out in the middle of the performance, crying, 'Excuse me, ladies and gentlemen, but I have a secret assignation in the woods with Frederica Hadley.' "

Frederica gave a gurgle of laughter. "I would be doomed."

"Let us sit down. What have you been doing?"

"Very little. Reading. Sewing for the poor."

She tugged at her gown. “I must begin to sew for myself.”

“Your sisters’ rejects?”

“Yes, my lord.”

“Do you not have gowns of your own?”

“No.”

“Why?”

“Because I lack looks, I am not considered worth the money.”

“I have already told you that you most certainly do not lack looks.”

“Thank you. There is great disappointment in my family because they have not seen you, except briefly at church, and must rely on servants’ gossip for news of you.”

“I have the feeling that it would be regarded with disfavor by my hosts should I suggest a call on the rectory.”

“Not only that. If you find Townley Hall boring, then you would find a visit to the rectory stultifying.”

“How so?”

“As I explained, I would need to show you my watercolors and Mary would read you some of her poetry.”

“Is Mary a good poet?”

“I do not think so, but perhaps I am not a very good judge.”

“Do you remember any of her poetry?”

“Yes, once I have heard something, it seems in my brain forever. I never forget anything.”

“Recite me some.”

"Her latest composition is called 'The Contented Soldier.' "

"Begin."

"I hear the raindrops patt'ring fast
Upon my canvass'd roof;
I see it bending to the blast,
But still 'tis tempest proof.

And as upon my bed of straw
Expecting sleep I lie,
I fear no fragile casement's flaw,
My bed is warm and dry.

Dear to me that humble bed
When tir'd with Duty's call;
For sweet the soldier's sleep can be,
If Conscience does not gall.

Then give the great their beds of down,
And Affluence all its charms;
The morning shall not see me frown
When Duty calls to arms."

There was a long silence when Frederica had finished. Then Lord Granton said, "That was truly wonderful."

"Oh dear, you do like her work!"

"No, I mean it is truly wonderfully awful. Does she write much?"

"Reams and reams. But I should not be cattish about Mary's poetry. It does scan to a certain extent. I suppose I am so used to being considered the inferior one that I am delighted to hear criticism of my own sister. Quite shabby in me."

"But oh so human. What are you reading these days?"

"About there being little difference between men and women."

"There is quite a difference, as you will find out when you are older. Who says there is no difference?"

"It was an article in the *Edinburgh Review.*"

"I am surprised the rectory not only allows you to read such an intelligent publication but pays for it, too."

"Oh no, Mama takes the *Ladies' Magazine* for the embroidery patterns, and the article was reprinted there."

"And how did this learned article come to the conclusion that the sexes are the same?"

"They argue that the difference in the masculine mind and the feminine mind arises simply through different training. They say that although they doubt that women should learn everything that men learn, there is no need for such great disparity in education between the sexes. They said that there is no just reason why a woman of forty should be more ignorant than a boy of twelve. Women — and this is so true — are excluded from all the serious business of the world. Men are lawyers, physicians, clergymen, apothecaries, and justices of the peace —

positions, they point out, that require less effort than rearing and suckling children, so why should not women be employed in the professions? You see," went on Frederica eagerly, "daughters are kept to occupations in sewing, patching, and mantua-making and, therefore, kept with nimble fingers and vacant minds."

"That is a very revolutionary idea."

"It is simply new, that is all." Frederica tugged at his sleeve for emphasis. "Do you not see? A century ago, who would have believed that country gentlemen could be brought to read and spell with the accuracy they do now?"

"I shall play devil's advocate," said Lord Granton. "It is said that the effect of knowledge is to make women pedantic and affected."

"That is because it is so rare, my lord. All affectation and display proceed from the supposition of possessing something better than the rest of the world possesses. Nobody is vain of possessing two arms and two legs. Diffuse knowledge among women and you will at once cure the conceit which knowledge occasions while it is rare."

"Now that is saying that a dandy should be aware his clothes are more expensive than anyone else's and parade them accordingly, and yet a vain man is regarded as a coxcomb."

Frederica bit her lip. "It says that there is a great deal of jealousy of learned women among pompous and foolish men."

"I gather from your father that you yourself

read a great deal of learned works. He does not protest?"

"I am not considered marriageable, so I may read what I like. Mary prides herself on her brain, but she confines herself to acceptable womanly pursuits like writing poetry, painting watercolors, and designing tapestry."

He picked up a small stone and threw it in the pool. They watched the ripples spread out, sparkling under the rising moon.

He was sitting quite close to her. He could smell a light scent coming from her body, not a fashionable perfume, something sweet and summery.

"There is another thing you have quite forgot," he said. "If women are to be apothecaries and lawyers and so forth, how do they find time to raise children and run a household?"

"You see, they would be earning a wage and could pay someone to do all that for them!"

"If you carry that argument to its logical conclusion, they will want someone else to bear the children for them. I apologize! I did not mean to be coarse."

"It is all right, my lord. We are not in the drawing room now or we would not dare talk thus. I think perhaps the answer is not to marry at all. Only think!" She stretched her arms wide. "A world where women can earn money at respectable jobs and do not need to marry, do not need to be condemned to a lifetime of breeding."

"Is your conversation usually so indelicate?"

"Of course not! I am not going to apologize. If you wish me to be missish, then I will go home immediately."

"Perhaps you should go home now in any case. What if you are missed?"

"I will not be."

"What of your sisters, your mother, your maid?"

"My mother and my sisters do not talk to me much, and I do not have a lady's maid."

"So how do you come by all the books you read?"

"The previous rector was a great scholar. When he died, his family did not want his books. His wife complained that they collected dust, and so they were left behind. There is quite an extensive library."

"There must be an appreciation of literature in your family or they would have been thrown out."

"Mama thought some of them might be valuable, and so they were all, except for a few handsome calf-bound ones, consigned to a room off the cellar in the basement. It is warm and dry. I take my candle and go down there and periodically search for more treasures."

"Do you read novels?"

"Yes, my mother and sisters read those. I enjoy some of them very much indeed."

"You should be brought out," he said half to himself.

Frederica laughed. "There is no money to bring me out, and besides, we have been having an interesting discussion on the rights of women to have a good education and yet the only future you can see for me is marriage."

"You do not want to be a spinster!"

"Why not? There are worse fates. I could be married to someone I don't much like. Better to live at the rectory with my books for company. Do you plan to stay long?"

"Not very much longer. I would have left before this, but my friend, Major Delisle, likes it here."

"So you are not going to propose to Annabelle?"

"No, she doesn't suit."

Frederica sighed. "How easy it is to be a man. To be able to pick and choose, to say this one won't suit, that one will, rather like a cattle auction."

"The ladies have their say. You should see some of the great beauties at the Season, playing one man off against the other."

"But they do not have the final say. When it comes to the matter of which one they should wed, the parents have the last word. Miss Beauty might be pining for a half-pay army captain as she meets Lord Thingummy at the altar. Then after they are married and a son is secured, Lord Thingummy will return to the arms of his mistress, and Lady Thingummy, jaded and neglected, takes the army captain as a lover."

"You have been reading the wrong books!"

"Do you mean it is not so?"

"In some cases, yes, but not all."

Frederica suddenly went very still. He would have spoken, but she held up her hand for silence. Then she murmured, "There is someone in these woods."

"How can you tell?" he whispered. "I hear nothing."

She got to her feet. "I must go. There is a presence here. I can sense it."

"Wait! I shall see you again, before I go. The day after tomorrow?"

"Very well, my lord. But earlier, please."

She turned and ran away lightly through the trees.

Lord Granton stayed where he was, straining every nerve to see if he could detect a watcher. But the wood was very quiet.

At last he rose and headed out of the wood.

Behind an oak tree, poacher Jack Muir heaved a sigh of relief. But as he, too, walked home with two rabbits concealed in the back pocket of his coat, he wondered what was going on with that pair. Miss Frederica from the rectory he knew by sight. She had called the man "my lord." It was probably that Lord Granton who was staying at Townley Hall. His slow brain turned the information over and over in his mind, wondering if there was any money to be made out of it.

The following day Lord Granton and the major

were out driving through the village with their hosts. As they passed the church, Lord Granton said suddenly, "Why do we not call on the rector?"

"He is probably out on his parish rounds," Annabelle said quickly.

"Shall we see, nonetheless?" Lord Granton said pleasantly, and with obvious reluctance, Sir Giles called to the coachman to stop.

Lord Granton heard a piercing scream from the rectory and wondered if someone had met with an accident.

But it was Mrs. Hadley, who had looked out the window of an upstairs room to witness their arrival and had screamed with alarm and surprise. For days and days she and Mary, Amy, and Harriet had been dressed in their finest, sitting, waiting, striking various Attitudes in the drawing room, but on this day they had given up hope. Amy and Harriet were still in bed, and Mary was mixing messes in the stillroom, and Mrs. Hadley herself was still in her undress.

She darted into Amy's room and then Harriet's, screaming that they must rise and dress in *minutes*. "Lord Granton is here! He is arrived!"

Down in the stillroom, Mary heard this and dropped a bottle of lavender water to the floor, where it splintered.

Meanwhile the company were being led into the drawing room by a little maid.

"Just listen to the fuss abovestairs," said Annabelle with a smile. "We have come at a bad moment."

"Exactly, my dear," said Lady Crown. "I think we should leave."

Lord Granton frowned. "I think the fuss is because they are making ready for our call. It would be most rude to leave now." He leaned back in an armchair and crossed his legs.

Finally the door opened, and a breathless and flurried Mrs. Hadley came in.

"You must have tea," she gasped after curtsying all round. "Yes, tea. Such another hot day. Quite tropical."

"There is no need," said Annabelle. "Lord Granton was desirous to speak to Dr. Hadley, but as he is obviously not here . . ."

"But he will be back any minute," said Mrs. Hadley, and then screamed at the maid, "Don't stand there gawking, girl. Tea! Tea!"

Annabelle raised her eyes to heaven, then shot a rueful look at Lord Granton.

Amy, Harriet, and Mary came in. Amy and Harriet were in white muslin, Mary in lilac silk. And Mary, Annabelle noticed with a sinking heart, was carrying a sheaf of what looked like poetry.

"So there are my beauties," said Mrs. Hadley proudly after the introductions had been made.

"And Miss Frederica?" asked Lord Granton.

"I am sure she is about somewhere," said Mrs. Hadley vaguely. "Always wandering, that girl."

"I have written a poem in honor of your arrival," said Mary, stepping forward.

"Oh, please," complained Annabelle, "I am sure Lord Granton is eager to be on his way."

But Lord Granton wanted to wait a little longer to see if Frederica made her appearance and so he said, "I would be charmed to hear it."

Mary took up a stance in the middle of the room. Harriet and Amy reclined in various Attitudes on the sofa.

" 'To Friendship,' " began Mary.

She cleared her throat and read her poem.

"Spring of delight! My muse would fain
Present a tribute to thy name:
Thy name belov'd by all!
Thy smile benign can soften pains:
Before thee Slav'ry drops her chains;
Fear ceases to appal.

Oh! May I always feel thy pow'r
Companion of the rural bow'r,
Thou sweetener of life;
I ask no greater bliss below,
Thy presence makes my bosom glow,
Dear banisher of strife!

Absence can never break the bands
When Love and Friendship join their hands;
The only foil is death:
Nor can he long the vict'ry claim,
They will above renew the same,
And dwell in firmer faith."

This was received in a polite silence. The major cleared his throat and said politely, "Jolly fine, that."

"Yes indeed," agreed Lord Granton. "I particularly like that bit about the glowing bosom."

Amy and Harriet giggled happily, but Mary preened and rustled her sheaf of papers. "I have another here," she began.

"Oh, spare us," snapped Annabelle. "You will bore our guests to extinction."

"Do sit down, Mary dear," her mother said hurriedly.

The door opened and Frederica walked in. She curtsied to the company and then went and sat on the window seat. Lord Granton noticed with some irritation that she was wearing that rather worn, rather large muslin gown he'd seen on her before.

"Have you been out walking, Miss Frederica?" he asked.

The rest of the company looked surprised that this distinguished guest should single out the least distinguished member.

"Yes, my lord," said Frederica.

"Ah, that is why you are wearing one of your old gowns."

Mrs. Hadley looked flustered and the rest of the young ladies, shocked.

"On the contrary, my lord," said Frederica, "this is my best gown. I saw the carriage and went upstairs to change."

Lord Granton took out his quizzing glass and

studied the finery of Frederica's sisters.

Then he tucked the quizzing glass away again. "I am flattered that you have gone to such effort for the company, Miss Frederica. I did not mean to appear rude. I was contrasting your gown with that of your sisters."

"We were just about to order a new wardrobe for Frederica," Mrs. Hadley rushed to say.

"I shall look forward to seeing the results," said Lord Granton. "Where did your walk take you, Miss Frederica?"

"One of the parishioners is sick. I was taking a jar of Mama's calve's-foot jelly to her."

Annabelle gave a little scream and pulled her skirts close. "Nothing infectious, I trust?"

"Ah, here is the tea tray," said Mrs. Hadley with obvious relief.

"Just typhoid," said Frederica.

"Typhoid!" screamed Annabelle. "Mama, Papa, we must leave."

Suddenly everyone seemed to be on their feet. Annabelle burst into tears and was led weeping from the room. Mrs. Hadley was shouting that there was no typhoid in the village, that Frederica had gone to see old Mrs. Partridge who was suffering from nothing less dire than a common cold.

Lord Granton glanced at Frederica quickly. He saw a gleam of amusement in her eyes. He bowed all round and followed his hosts from the room.

"You told a lie!" Mrs. Hadley screamed as

the carriage rumbled off.

"I was beginning to say that Mrs. Partridge, who is very nervous, thought she had the typhoid," said Frederica, looking the picture of innocence, "but I was able to persuade her it was only a common cold."

Mrs. Hadley found her voice. "Go to your room immediately, Frederica, until I think how to deal with you. Your father will need to go to the hall and explain matters. How could you, you bad, bad girl."

"Just because you are never likely to attract a man," said Mary waspishly, "you want to spoil things for the rest of us."

Lord Granton was not surprised to learn later that there was no typhoid whatsoever in the village, and he was amused. He wanted to see Frederica again and find out why she had told such a lie.

He sought out the major and told him that the typhoid scare was all a hum.

"Do you mean that little girl deliberately made it all up?" declared the major wrathfully. "Poor Miss Annabelle was quite overset."

"The story from the rector, who came up oiling and cringing, is that Frederica meant to say that Mrs. Partridge only thought she had the typhoid."

"And I think that odd little girl only said it to break up the party."

"Were you sorry? Had she not done so, we

might have had to endure another of Mary's poems."

"I thought the other Hadley girls were pretty and charming. There is something strange-looking about that Frederica. And why did you go on about her shabby gown? Not the thing at all to make personal comments like that."

"I was sorry for her," said Lord Granton. "I do not see why she cannot be as finely gowned as her sisters."

"The reason," said the major, still angry, "is because she is probably all about in her upper chambers. Lots of inbreeding in these villages."

"Come, now, I do not think our good rector married his first cousin, or anything like that. I believe Miss Frederica to be the most interesting person in this dull bit of the country."

"Some little rectory miss who is not even old enough to put her hair up and behaves in a farouche manner?"

"She is eighteen. She should have her hair up, and she should have a new gown."

The major looked at him doubtfully. "I have been persuading you to stay on. Perhaps I should take your suggestion and leave. Of course, there is this ball."

"What ball?"

"The ball in your honor," said the major. "It's to be held in two weeks' time. I told you all about it and so did the Crowns."

"I probably wasn't listening."

"I believe you are expected to announce your

engagement to Annabelle Crown at this ball."

"Never! We had best leave."

"Can't do that," said the major. "All the invitations have been out this age. You've made it pretty plain you don't like Miss Crown."

"I have been all that is polite!"

"But hardly the lover. So they cannot expect you to propose."

"I do not know about that," said Lord Granton slowly. "Annabelle is quite vain. I think that is why she did not take during her Season. She is very spoilt and makes no effort to please, and she has little conversation."

"Damning. But I cannot agree. I find her charming."

"Then you propose to her!"

The major walked across the room and studied himself in the mirror and then shook his head. "With my face and figure, I would not have a hope."

"You underrate yourself, Harry."

"We'll see. Anyway, Frederica has made it possible for the Crowns to say that the Hadley girls will not be welcome at the ball."

"That seems harsh."

"I do not see what you can do about it."

"I should be able to find a way. Where is Lady Crown?"

"In the drawing room. What are you going to do?"

"I'll think of something on my road there."

When he entered the drawing room, he found

the family assembled — Sir Giles, Lady Crown, and Annabelle.

"I am so sorry," he began. "I had quite forgot about your ball. I was about to announce my leave."

Annabelle's mouth fell open in dismay. Lady Crown said, "But you cannot leave! The ball is in your honor."

"It is my guilty conscience which makes me feel I must leave."

"What is the matter?" asked Sir Giles, finding his voice.

"Those poor girls from the rectory must have little in the way of a social life. I feel it is because of me that they have been told they cannot come."

"Frederica's behavior this day was disgraceful," protested Lady Crown.

"But I still feel guilty. I really should return to London."

"In that case," said Sir Giles, all forced jollity, "they may come."

"I am most grateful to you," said Lord Granton while Annabelle's mind worked busily. Why this interest in the welfare of the Hadley girls? The only one he had addressed was Frederica.

When the viscount had left, Lady Crown said fretfully, "I had best send one of the footmen over to the rectory with a letter."

"May I suggest, Mama," said Annabelle sweetly, "that since Frederica is the cause of all the trouble, she should be excluded as a just punishment."

"Yes, I think so," agreed Sir Giles. "There's something odd about that girl."

"Perhaps Lord Granton is a trifle eccentric," suggested Annabelle. "I do not think it necessary to tell him that Frederica is not invited. Good heavens, we are doing enough having the rest of them."

The rector gloomily took the letter from the Townley Hall footman. What now, he thought with a shudder. He had earlier received a letter telling him that he and his family were uninvited to the ball. He felt he was dwelling in a house of mourning. Frederica, as usual, was out walking. Her sisters and Mrs. Hadley were in their respective rooms.

He bleakly asked the footman if any reply was expected, and having been told none, waited until the footman had left and then gloomily cracked open the seal. He was sure it would contain nothing more than further recriminations on Frederica's behavior. It didn't.

He read it again slowly. His face lightened. He thought it a charming letter. They were to go after all. Lady Crown said she felt it unfair they should be punished over just one girl's rudeness. To that end, Frederica should still be excluded.

He rushed upstairs and entered his wife's bedroom. "Go away," she said faintly. "We are socially ruined."

"No, my dear," said the rector triumphantly. "Here is a delightful letter from Lady Crown re-inviting us."

"Oh, my stars!" cried Mrs. Hadley, raising herself from the bed on which she had been lying. "We must tell the girls."

"Wait!" He held up his hand. "There is one thing. Frederica is not to go."

"Then she will be receiving a much needed lesson."

There was a silence while both Frederica's parents thought about her iniquities.

Finally Mrs. Hadley said, "There is something *incalculable* about our youngest. Perhaps it might be diplomatic not to tell her she is not invited until the last minute."

"That seems cruel," protested the rector.

"But listen." Mrs. Hadley swung herself down from the high bed. "What if Lord Granton calls again? And what if Frederica should say something rude or awkward simply out of pique because she knows she has not been invited?"

The rector continued to protest for a few minutes but was not very forceful and soon found himself agreeing weakly to his wife's plan.

Mrs. Hadley, satisfied, rushed from the room to tell Frederica's elder sisters the glad news. But she did not tell them that Frederica was not to go to the ball. She feared that Mary might find it too tempting to crow over the younger girl because Mary was often jealous of Frederica's learning.

So when Frederica returned it was to find a festive air about the old rectory. She tried to tell herself that she was totally unaffected by the news. But deep in her heart was a bright little image of dancing with Lord Granton. She would insist on wearing her hair up and demand a new gown.

And then her face fell. She had never learned how to dance. Her sisters had been taught by an itinerant dancing master, but the lessons had not extended to her, and she had not minded very much at the time.

Now what was she to do?

Chapter Three

Lord Granton kept glancing at the clock over the mantel in the dining room. He could not keep pleading a headache in order to slip out and meet Frederica. He thought hard and as soon as the ladies had retired, he said to Sir Giles, "I must beg to be excused for the rest of the evening. I have been neglecting my writing."

"Didn't know you were a scholar," remarked Sir Giles, surprised. "What are you writing?"

"A novel."

"You surprise me! Novels are for the ladies."

"Men write novels, too. In fact I am basing this novel on my pleasant visit to Townley Hall. May I dedicate it to you and your family?"

"I am most gratified . . . honored," said Sir Giles. Wait until he told his wife and Annabelle about this! "Let me not delay you."

Lord Granton smiled sweetly and escaped upstairs, where he changed quickly out of his evening dress. A little stab of conscience told him he was behaving disgracefully in having secret assignations with a young virgin. If they were ever discovered, Frederica would land in the middle of a scandal.

But his desire to escape the stuffy surroundings

of Townley Hall overrode any pangs of conscience.

Soon he was hurrying off in the direction of the wood.

He stopped before he reached the pond. Frederica was there, pirouetting slowly in the moonlight. "What are you doing?" he called softly.

She turned round and said sadly, "I was wishing I could dance."

He came up to her. "You cannot dance?"

She shook her head. "I never learned. My sisters were taught by a dancing master, but it was not considered necessary for me to learn."

Lord Granton did not know that Frederica was to be excluded from the ball.

"You do seem to lack bottom," he complained. "I am sure had you insisted on being taught, your mother would have agreed."

"Perhaps," said Frederica on a sigh.

"There is nothing else for it. I will need to teach you myself."

"Where?"

"Here, I suppose. If we move back to that grassy glade, it will be our ballroom floor. Now, we will start with a simple country dance. You will need to imagine the other people in the set, say eight couples in all."

He began to hum a jaunty air in a strong baritone.

Frederica was too excited to observe that the situation was odd or amusing. And Lord Granton found her an apt pupil as they crossed and re-crossed in the figure of the dance over the springy turf.

"Enough," he said at last. "Next time we will try the quadrille."

"When can that be . . . the next time?"

"I have made an excuse that I am writing a novel based on my visit to Townley Hall."

"Which, of course, you are not."

"You know me well. I shall tell them I can work only in the evenings."

"I wonder if Mama will buy me a new gown for the ball. There is not time enough to have one made, but perhaps at the dressmakers' in Chipping Norton they might have something."

"I should think anything Chipping Norton has to offer would be sadly provincial."

"Not at all. Miss Hendry has retired from London, and she is very clever and still very expensive."

"And you think Mrs. Hadley will comply?"

"I can only ask. There is a book in the library at Townley Hall which describes the various figures and steps of dances. I overheard Annabelle talking about it one day."

"If I can find it, I will bring it tomorrow." He hesitated. "We must make sure we are not surprised, Frederica. No one must know of our meetings."

She looked at him innocently. "I most certainly would not dream of telling anyone."

"Now, I want to know why you told that

dreadful lie about Mrs. Partridge having typhoid."

"Oh, you knew I was lying."

"Of course, you dreadful brat."

"I saw Mary with her poems and I knew if I did not do something, you would be trapped forever and Sir Giles would be furious with my father."

"But as it was, everyone was furious with you!"

"I am truly sorry to have alarmed everyone. I have never behaved quite so wantonly before. It is the boredom, you see."

"Try not to be so wicked again or you will all be banned from the ball, and how can I dance with you if you are not there?"

Frederica looked at him, her eyes glowing in the moonlight. "Oh, I should like that above all things!"

He wondered uneasily whether she might be falling in love with him, but her next remark reassured him.

"You must dance two whole dances with me. I have never been able to put the ladies' noses out of joint before. I have never had anyone jealous of me. It would be a new experience."

"And you will be strong and ask for a new ball gown?"

"Yes, I will be strong."

"Then, my chuck, as the ball will soon be upon us, I will meet you again here tomorrow night. But make sure you are not discovered!"

Frederica smiled at him. "I am very careful."

She curtsied to him and moved away quickly through the trees. He waited for a few minutes beside the pool and then began to make his own way out of the wood.

He heard a twig crack behind him and swung around. A man detached himself from the shadow of a tree trunk at the edge of the wood.

"Who are you?" demanded the viscount harshly.

The man approached. "I be Jack Muir, my lord."

"And what do you mean by creeping after me?"

"Reckon it would cause a bit of a scandal, my lord, if I were to tell 'em up at the Hall that you'd been meeting young miss from the rectory on the sly, like."

Lord Granton stood with his hands on his hips and surveyed Jack. He could see his features clearly in the moonlight, the crafty eyes, the stubbled chin, the long coat with the large bulging pocket that he wore despite the warmth of the summer's evening.

"It is all very simple, fellow," drawled Lord Granton. "You tell them at the Hall about my innocent meetings and I will tell how you were found in these woods with your pocket bulging with dead rabbits. If you are lucky, you will only be transported, but you know the stringency of the game laws. You probably will be hanged."

Jack began to back off. "I meant no harm.

Look, my lord, I say nothing about you, and you don't say nothing about me."

"If I find you skulking about these woods again," said Lord Granton, "then I may tell Sir Giles about you before I leave. Be off with you!"

Another twig cracked and Jack melted back into the shadows. Lord Granton walked around the edge of the field, where a light breeze moved through the wheat, which was silvery in the moonlight, like Frederica's hair.

He felt naked and exposed and that the countryside was full of secret, watching eyes.

He should not meet her again. He would find an excuse to call at the rectory the following afternoon and convey to her that their pleasant, secret conversations were over.

Boredom like a black cloud settled round him. He gained the road and strode down it, looking every inch the devil he was reported to be.

To his relief, Annabelle proved to be suffering from a summer cold the following day, and not wanting Lord Granton to see her with red eyes and a running nose had kept to her room, so a planned expedition to the nearest town of Evesham to view the abbey was canceled.

To his hosts' demands that they do something else to entertain their guests, he replied he would prefer to go out for a walk alone and think what to write in the next chapter.

He decided to walk to the rectory but regretted his decision when he reached the lodge at the west gate of the estate. The sun was fiercer than ever, and sad little yellow dried-up leaves pattered down from the trees over his head. The hot summer was producing an unnatural sort of autumn. Dried leaves crunched under his feet as he strode along the road. White dust rose about him. When he reached the village, he noticed that the level in the village pond had dropped considerably.

The golden Cotswold stone of the cottages seemed to absorb the sunlight into their already hot walls.

He pushed open the gate to the rectory and walked along the winding path to the low old door, which stood open. He pulled the bell. A little maid came running. "Oh, my lord," she said, bobbing a curtsy, "Dr. Hadley is on his parish rounds, and the ladies are gone to Chipping Norton."

So Frederica had succeeded in her desire for a dress. He nodded his thanks and turned away. But then he heard singing from abovestairs and turned back to where the maid still stood at the open door.

"Who is that singing?" he asked.

"Oh, that's Miss Frederica."

"I thought you said no one was at home!"

"I do beg your pardon, my lord. I forgot about Miss Frederica," said the maid, Bessie, who had not forgotten at all, but did not rate Frederica as being important enough to receive the viscount.

"Then," said Lord Granton patiently, "would you be so good as to tell Miss Frederica that I am called?"

"Yes, indeed, my lord." The maid looked flustered. "Do step inside, my lord, and I will fetch her."

She ushered Lord Granton into the rectory drawing room.

After a few minutes the door opened and Frederica came in. She was wearing an old gown, blue muslin this time, which was so short, it showed her ankles.

"If I had been warned you meant to call," said Frederica crossly, "I would have put on another gown."

"My apologies. Can we talk without being overheard?"

"I will fetch my bonnet. We will take a walk. In this old house there are so many chimneys and holes in the floors that one can hear everything."

Frederica left and came back shortly with a wide shady bonnet on her head.

"I am going over to the church with Lord Granton, Bessie," said Frederica. "He is anxious to view the crusader's tomb."

"Were you always such a liar?" he asked.

"I never think of it as lying," said Frederica equably. "I have always considered it being diplomatic. The church might be a good idea after all, my lord. It is about the only cool place for miles around."

He opened the heavy church door for her and they walked into the greenish gloom. "No stained glass," he remarked. "Cromwell's soldiers, I suppose."

"Yes. Barton Sub Edge suffered just like everywhere else. I am glad I did not live then."

"I am sure you would have enjoyed it all immensely, Miss Frederica, and would have hidden fleeing cavaliers in the basement of the rectory."

She turned to face him. "Did you come to see me?"

He nodded. "Our meetings have been discovered."

She turned quite pale.

"Do not look so frightened. It was only a poacher."

"Jack Muir?"

"The same." He told her of his meeting with Muir.

"I think he hoped to make money out of it," said Lord Granton. "The silly fool forgot that although he might be able to create a scandal, I could get him hanged."

"So we shall not meet again." Frederica's voice was very low, and he had to bend his head to hear her.

"Perhaps that would be wise." He searched in a pocket of his coat and brought out a small book. "But here is the book giving the figures of all the dances that you wanted. You must teach yourself the rest."

"Thank you."

"And you will wear your new gown and your hair up and be the belle of the ball."

"I am not to get a new gown, my lord."

"Indeed! I assumed that was why your mama had gone to Chipping Norton."

"No, my lord. I broached the subject and my suggestion was met with such fury. I do not know why it should have upset Mama so much. She said that Amy's old ball gown was perfectly suitable. And so it is. But it is not mine, if you take my meaning."

Not knowing that Frederica was not supposed to attend the ball, Lord Granton found himself becoming very angry indeed over what he considered Mrs. Hadley's unnatural cruelty and parsimony.

Instead he remarked, "I shall miss our meetings."

"As shall I." Frederica bent her head so that the wide brim of her straw hat shaded her face. "It will somehow make it harder to go back to my quiet life. Is it because you fear Jack might talk after all?"

"No, I do not think he will dare. But I would always feel there was someone among the trees, spying and listening."

"There are other places," murmured Frederica.

He looked down at her disconsolate little figure. If he did not escape in the evenings to meet her anymore, he would be condemned to those long, stuffy, boring evenings listening to Annabelle either prattle or play the harp.

He knew he should not reply, that he should simply bow and wish her well, promise her those two dances, and take his leave.

He found himself saying, "Where, for instance?"

"Come and I will show you. If we are surprised by any member of my family, it will not look odd. There is a pretty stream near here."

"Then let us go and look at it."

The sun struck down on them when they emerged from the church. As they walked through the village, Frederica nodded to various people, conscious of the speculative stares.

"Not causing too much comment, I hope?" he asked.

She shook her head. "I am not old enough or pretty enough to cause comment. They no doubt think I am taking you to see my father. We go this way, my lord." She climbed nimbly over a stile without waiting for him and began to cross a meadow. He followed her, taking off his hat and coat and carrying them.

The field was carpeted in wildflowers. In front of him, Frederica's fine, fair hair streamed down her back under the sunbonnet, and her gown was as blue as the sky above. He experienced a rare feeling of well-being, of comfort.

More woods lay ahead but not, he hoped, any watching poachers.

It was a fir wood, the trees, tall and scented, forming a pillared alley that twisted and turned its way toward the stream, which he could now hear rushing along.

He emerged from the trees to stand beside Frederica on an open space of green grass starred with daisies beside the stream, which foamed and tumbled over rocks at their feet.

"This doesn't seem to have been affected by the heat," he said.

"No," agreed Frederica, taking off her hat and sitting down on the grass. "It is fed by springs and is the lifeline of the village."

He sat down beside her and together they looked at the racing water. At last he said, "If I meet you here tonight, do you think anyone will come across us?"

"Not here," she said seriously. "It is haunted."

"By whom?"

"By Miss Abigail Bentley."

"And who was Miss Abigail Bentley?"

"It is such a sad story," said Frederica. "She was a spinster of this parish, quite old, about thirty-four, I believe. Oh, I am sorry, my lord, but it seems old to me. In any case, the story runs — this was about fifty years ago — that there was a certain Mr. Tarrant who came as a guest to Townley Hall. He was very fashionable. He wore the latest in powdered wigs, satin waistcoats, embroidered coats, and those shoes you see in old portraits of macaronis with high red heels. Miss Abigail was a gentlewoman who lived on a small allowance from a family trust. She did not receive enough to live comfortably but managed in a sort of genteel poverty. She was not reputed to be particularly pretty. The old people said her great beauty was in her hair, which was thick and glossy and brown.

"There was a fair in the village and that was where Mr. Tarrant came across her. They fell into conversation and soon they began to be seen going for walks together. Miss Bentley is reported to have become briefly beautiful because she was so much in love. Then she was seen wearing a brand-new silk gown. The then rector, a Dr. Pierrepoint, became anxious for Miss Bentley's reputation. He begged her to be careful, as Mr. Tarrant was only dallying with her, but she replied flatly that Mr. Tarrant was as much in love with her as she was with him and they were to be married.

"The good rector approached Mr. Tarrant. Mr. Tarrant became very haughty and said the rector ought to be horsewhipped for questioning him on a personal matter.

"That night one of the villagers saw Mr. Tarrant enter Miss Bentley's cottage. In the morning he was gone: gone entirely from the Hall, gone from the village. But Miss Bentley still glowed with love, that was until a letter arrived for her a week later. What it said, no one ever knew, though they did know the letter had been delivered, and her neighbors heard a great rending scream.

"On the following morning she was found floating in the pool, just above here. She had thrown herself in. She left a note to say that Mr. Tarrant had betrayed her, that she was ruined.

"Poor Miss Bentley was buried at the cross-roads with a stake through her heart."

There was a silence while both Frederica and Lord Granton contemplated the barbaric way that suicides were buried to stop their ghosts walking.

"And yet her ghost walks," he said at last.

"So they say, but I have never seen her."

"And are you not frightened to come here?"

"I have nothing to fear from the poor, lost ghost of Miss Bentley."

"You have your own kind of courage, Frederica."

"Thank you, my lord."

"You may call me Rupert, as we are friends."

Frederica turned her face away to hide the sudden glow of happiness that shone there. And then, almost unbidden, came the thought of Miss Bentley. Had Mr. Tarrant praised her and flattered her and made some silly village woman think he might want to marry her? But Lord Granton had not made any advances to her, Frederica, nor had he flirted with her. In fact, he talked to her as he would to a young man.

The glow left her face and she stared at the rushing water.

"Why so quiet?" came his voice.

"I was thinking of Miss Bentley."

"She is dead and gone, lady. Think of all the dead around this countryside, thousands and thousands."

"You are right. I shall think of something pleasant. Will you teach me more dancing to-night?"

"I will try. But you seem to be an apt pupil. Perhaps I should leave now."

"Yes, I think you should. For the news will surely have reached Papa now that you called, and he will be hunting everywhere."

They both rose. He raised her hand to his lips.

"Good-bye, Frederica."

"Good-bye, Rupert."

She stood by the stream for a long time after he had gone, holding the hand he had kissed against her cheek, a dreamy smile on her lips.

When Frederica eventually entered her home it was to find it in an uproar. "What is this?" cried Mrs. Hadley. "Lord Granton called and none of us here?"

"I was here," said Frederica calmly. "He wished to see the church and so I took him there."

"But what did he *say?*" screamed Amy. "Did he talk of Annabelle? Did he ask for any of us?"

"No, he stayed but a few minutes, sent his regards to Papa, and went on his way."

"How infuriating. Only you in that shabby gown," complained Mrs. Hadley.

"Lord Granton is used to seeing me in shabby

gowns," said Frederica.

"As to that," said Mrs. Hadley, "I bought two lengths of pretty sprigged muslin in Chipping Norton. Mrs. Pomfrey can make you up at least three new gowns."

"Mrs. Pomfrey makes everything look fussy and provincial," said Frederica.

"There's gratitude for you!" said her mother, raising her eyes to heaven, and starting to cry.

"I am sorry," said Frederica awkwardly. "I am indeed most ungrateful, and it is most kind of you, Mama."

Mrs. Hadley swept off up the stairs, still crying. Frederica did not know that her mother was becoming increasingly plagued with guilt as the days before the ball slipped by. She had begun to dread telling Frederica she could not go.

Major Harry Delisle was waiting for his friend when Lord Granton returned.

"Where have you been? The family has been asking for you."

"I went to look at the church."

"But you saw it on Sunday."

"I like looking at churches when they are empty."

"You've changed. And what's this rubbish about writing a book?"

Lord Granton gave his friend a limpid look. "On the contrary, it is not rubbish."

"Well, it must be. I mean, based on Townley

Hall! You have radiated boredom since we got here."

"It is that very boredom which has prompted me to do something constructive."

"And so you are really writing a book?"

"Yes, I am really writing a book. I find I can write only in the evenings, hence my abrupt departure from the dinner table."

"I thought I knew you," grumbled the major. "You were always gallant whether the lady bored you or not, and there's Miss Annabelle with a cold and you have never sent her your regards."

"She is not dying, my friend."

"I still say you have changed. There is a secrecy about you."

"It is the heat. This dreadful heat which goes on and on."

The major continued to look at him suspiciously. Then he said, "I have a mind to settle down. I have a mind to propose to Miss Annabelle."

"Then I would do so after the ball."

"Why?"

"Because," said Lord Granton patiently, "despite my indifference and coldness, I know they expect me to propose at the ball, to make an announcement. The Crowns are the type of people who see only the title. Should you propose when they are sharp with disappointment, then you will be accepted."

"Good idea," cried the major, rubbing his chubby hands.

"But," went on Lord Granton, "is it any use in my pointing out that you are worth better, Harry, than being accepted simply because the Crowns' ambitions have been thwarted?"

"I am used to being considered second best," said the major in a low voice. "I do not have your title, your dangerous reputation, or your elegance."

"I still say you are worth more. After your marriage you will have to listen to Annabelle playing the harp every damn evening."

"I can think of nothing more blissful," said the major quietly.

"I do believe you are in love."

The major heaved a sigh. "I do believe I am."

The heat in the dining room at Townley Hall that evening was suffocating. Annabelle, slightly red about the nose, was fanning herself languidly. No breeze stirred the curtains at the open windows.

She covertly studied Lord Granton. Anxious to see what was in this book he was writing, she had searched his room while he was out without finding a single scrap of paper. Was he so bored that he was merely claiming to be writing a book as an excuse to cut short his evenings? Arrogant and vain as she was, that thought buried itself like a worm in Annabelle's brain.

"How goes your writing?" she asked the viscount.

"Tolerably well, Miss Annabelle." His face was

saturnine and his eyes glinted oddly in the candlelight. Annabelle thought he looked mocking and said with an edge in her voice, "You must let us see some of your work. No one has seen any evidence of it."

"I am shy," drawled Lord Granton, twisting the stem of his wineglass. My room has been searched, he thought furiously. My man was sure someone had been going through my belongings. "In fact," he went on, "I am so shy that every day I give my work to my man, Gustave, and tell him to keep it under lock and key."

Vanity and common sense warred in Annabelle's brain and vanity won. Her parents had convinced her that Lord Granton was sure to propose to her before or at the ball, and in these days of correct manners, it was surely not at all odd that he had not shown much warmth toward her. So when he rose at the end of the meal and made his usual apologies, she was able to watch him depart with complacency. She might not have been so complacent had his friend, the major, not been so gallant in his attentions to her. With Major Delisle praising her and hanging on her every word, Annabelle felt secure in her attractions.

Lord Granton escaped from the Hall and made his way through the estate by a route that would not be overlooked from the front of the hall where the drawing room and dining room faced. He was wearing black: black coat, black breeches, and black leather top boots. He did not want to be seen. He skirted the village by a circuitous route. The air was so close and so stifling he was sure the villagers would be standing outside their doors to catch any breath of air the evening might afford. For one moment his stride faltered and he wondered what on earth he was doing putting Frederica's reputation at risk.

Then he shrugged and walked on. She was the only person who had amused him in ages. Without him she would not know how to dance at the ball.

He found her sitting on the grass beside the river and sank down beside her with a little sigh of relief. "This must be the only cool place for miles around. We will talk for a bit and then we will dance. How did you fare this day?"

"Mama and my sisters were vastly disappointed to have missed you, but Mama has bought me muslin for new gowns. The only problem is they are to be made by our village dressmaker and so they will look, well, *villagy*."

"But nothing suitable for a ball gown?"

"No, and there is something odd there. If I talk about the ball, Mama closes up and changes the subject. I suppose it is because she still blames me for nearly causing their invitations to be canceled."

"Are you not a good needlewoman?"

"I am fair enough, but not nearly good enough to fashion a ball gown."

"Perhaps if you say your prayers, something will happen."

"I think the good Lord has more to do than listen to one vain village miss asking for a ball gown."

"You will never know until you try."

"I never thought to be urged to say my prayers by the devil himself."

"Alas, my reputation! Now, Frederica, this is going to be a complicated dance tonight. The quadrille."

Frederica got to her feet. "A French chalked ballroom floor will appear luxury after trying to dance on grass."

He marched her first through the intricate figures of the dance and then showed her the steps. "Some members of society even have ballet masters to teach them entrechats, but I do not think you should attempt anything so daring."

"Have you performed the waltz?" asked Frederica.

"Of course. It has not yet been sanctioned by Almack's, that holy of holies."

"I would like to go to Almack's assembly rooms just once," said Frederica wistfully. "Are they very grand?"

"The company is but the rooms are nothing out of the common way, and the fare is lemonade and rather stale sandwiches. One goes there to be seen."

"And to find a husband?"

"Yes, the rooms hold the most expensive marriage market in the world."

Frederica half closed her eyes. "I can imagine

it. My Lord Granton arrives. There is a flutter among the debutantes. Which will be the lucky one? Lord Granton has an evil reputation and looks like the devil, but no matter. There is the title and fortune to consider, and Mama and Papa would be so pleased and the other ladies so jealous."

He smiled down at her. "And my charms have nothing to do with this flutter?"

"I should not think so," said Frederica, wrinkling her smooth brow. "Perhaps the married ladies anxious for an affair may view you thus."

"You should not be so cynical at such a young age."

"I did not mean to be rude. There are times when I forget exactly to whom I am talking."

He had a sudden desire to flirt with her, to see her become aware of him as a man, but he fought down the impulse.

The night was too warm and calm and innocent. The water foamed over the rocks in the stream. The faintest of breezes sprang up and rattled the dry leaves of a stand of birch. Moonlight silvered the grass and the stars burned overhead.

"I must go," he said suddenly.

Frederica's eyes were large in the darkness. "I *have* offended you, Rupert."

"No, I will return tomorrow night. I do not want our country idyll to end just yet." Again he raised her hand to his lips and kissed it.

She waited by the stream, watching him until

he had disappeared. She felt suddenly sad. Soon he would leave and life in the sleepy village would never be quite the same. A treacherous feeling of discontent took hold of her. If only she were older, richer, beautiful, then there would be no reason for the idyll, as he had called it, ever to end.

The newspapers were avidly perused by Mrs. Hadley, not for news of the war in the Peninsula but for royal gossip, marriages, and engagements. She liked to read the juicier pieces aloud.

Frederica entered the drawing room the next morning in time to hear her mother exclaim, "Do but hear this. A certain Lord M. who is in his forties has been forced to wed a Miss C. who is but eighteen. He was staying in the country somewhere at the village of J. I do hate these initials. Why do they not come out and say who the people are? It seems this Lord M. was in the way of secretly meeting this Miss C., who was not of his rank but merely the daughter of a gentleman farmer. The villagers came to learn of their secret meetings and told Miss C.'s parents. Lord M. protested — and do but hear this — that the girl amused him and he had only been enlivening an otherwise boring visit. Miss C.'s parents insist he marry her. He says he has done nothing wrong and is refusing to do so. Have you ever heard anything so ridiculous? Miss C. weeps and protests her innocence and says they only talked."

"No one is going to believe that, Mama," said Mary.

"It all sounds reasonable to me," said Frederica, a knot of fear forming in her stomach.

"You poor innocent," retorted Mrs. Hadley, rattling the newspaper. "When you are older and wiser to the ways of the world, you will know that middle-aged men do not dally in the countryside with young misses for the benefit of their conversation."

Lord Granton had shown no interest in her as a woman, thought Frederica. But what if they were discovered? She bit her lip in vexation. He would survive the scandal. It would add to his reputation, but it would ruin hers.

She would not meet him that evening, or any other evening. She could not write and tell him so; she dared not.

She wandered up to her room and sat wearily in a chair by the window. Perhaps he would be offended and he would not dance with her at the ball.

At last she rose. She decided to go back to the pool where she had first met him. It would not matter if anyone saw her. She would be alone.

She slipped out by the back stairs, feeling the heat of the sun burning through the thin muslin of her gown. She looked up at the glaring, remorseless cloudless blue of the sky. The old people in the village said they could remember summers like this in their youth, but Dr. Hadley had shaken his head and said there had never been a summer like this. Old people, looking back, only remembered the sunny days.

When she entered the wood and headed for the pool, she suddenly stopped, aware that she was not alone.

She was not afraid. Barton Sub Edge had been remarkably free of the footpads and highwaymen that haunted other parts of England.

But she looked around and said loudly, "Who's there?"

Jack Muir, the poacher, came out from behind a tree.

"What do you want?" asked Frederica. "Why are you hiding like that?"

Jack came up to her, a big grin on his face. He was holding a parcel. "A certain gennelman said I could make myself useful by givin' you this."

He handed her the square parcel wrapped in tissue paper.

Jack had been hailed by Lord Granton earlier in the day. He had been given a couple of sovereigns and told to find Frederica when no one else was around and to give her the parcel. Jack, delighted to have made money out of this lord somehow, had lurked about the rectory until he saw Frederica leave and had followed her.

"Thank you," said Frederica, coloring up.

He touched his forelock and slid away quietly through the trees. Frederica sat down in the grass with the parcel on her lap and then slowly opened it. There was a folded letter on top under the wrappings. She cracked the seal. "Please do me the honor of accepting this ball gown, Frederica. Your humble servant, Rupert."

She shook out the ball gown and held it up. It was of white muslin embroidered with seed pearls. It had a low square neck. Silver embroidery and seed pearls encrusted the bodice. It was a miracle of stitching and design. She stared at it, her heart beating hard. Had he run mad? How could she tell her mother about the gown?

Her fingers trembled as they ran lightly over the embroidery. But it was so beautiful. What could she do? For the present she would hide it in her room. Perhaps she could pretend to be altering Amy's gown, the one she was supposed to wear, and then brazen it out on the evening of the ball and swear all the work was her own. But where was she supposed to have found all those pearls and silver for the embroidery? A tear rolled down her cheek. She would need to meet him that evening and ask his advice.

Once more at the Blackstones', Lord Granton made easy conversation as all the while he worried and worried about that gown. On impulse he had driven to Chipping Norton and to that dressmaker that Frederica had told him about, where he was told about a lady who had asked for a ball gown to be made and then had not collected it. He saw it and knew somehow it would fit Frederica perfectly. And meeting that villain, Jack, on the road home had been too much of a temptation. Jack could not betray him, but what if Frederica thought he had gone too far and told her parents? The heat was adding to his temper and worry. Lady Blackstone had a high, fluting voice that grated on his nerves. Furthermore, on walks about the estate, Annabelle had adopted the habit of taking his arm in a possessive sort of way that was obviously causing the jealous major some distress.

Would the long hot day never end?

The Blackstones had other company, two plain girls and their parents. The girls had obviously been told that Lord Granton was Annabelle's property, and he began to feel trapped. If it were not for Frederica, he would run away before that wretched ball.

As they were approaching the gazebo, Annabelle clutching his arm, the rest of the company walking behind, Lord Granton said testily, "I do not wish to be ungallant, Miss Annabelle, but it is much too hot to walk arm in arm." He detached himself. "I am sorry," said Annabelle, tossing her head. "Perhaps I should ask the major to accompany me."

"Perhaps you should," said Lord Granton angrily. He strode on ahead, leaving Annabelle staring after him.

Had the major not been so softhearted, Annabelle and her parents might have realized at last that there was no hope whatsoever of a proposal from Lord Granton at the ball or at any other time. But the major, hurrying up to the distressed Annabelle, saw the tears in her eyes and could not bear to know his beloved suffered, so he said, "You must forgive my friend. He never could stand the heat. Besides, having escaped marriage for so long, the thought of being shackled makes him testy."

Annabelle, from looking the very picture of a distressed maiden, became quite radiant. "Oh, you gentlemen." She giggled, rapping his arm with the sticks of her fan. "How are we poor ladies to know where we stand?"

She lost no time in abandoning the major to whisper to her mother that Granton really meant to propose and that his crusty behavior was only due to nerves at the prospect of becoming married at last. The major had said so, and who should know better than his best friend?

Lord Granton, suddenly aware of the smiles of approval being thrown at him by the Crown family, wondered vaguely what it was all about, but was not interested enough to find out.

He located Frederica that evening sitting by the river, the tissue paper–wrapped dress on her knees. He sank down beside her.

"It is very beautiful," said Frederica sadly, fingering the tissue paper. "But how can I wear it? Where was such an expensive gown supposed to come from?"

"Could you not say you made it?"

Frederica gave a bleak little laugh. "Where on earth could I say I found all those seed pearls and the silver for the embroidery?"

"Do you not have any rich relative, any indulgent rich relative?"

"There is a distant relative of Papa's, a Lady Prebend, but she is so very distant, something a hundred times removed."

"I knew Lady Prebend. She died two months ago, as I recall."

"So that is that."

"Does your family know she is dead?"

"No, nothing was mentioned."

"Then there is your answer. Give me the gown and I will have it delivered to you tomorrow with a letter supposed to come from Lady Prebend. She was accounted eccentric and they will know that."

Frederica's eyes shone with hope. "But what will happen should they ever find out she is dead?"

"You must just shake your pretty head and say the old lady must have left instructions for the gown to be sent to you and it must have been forwarded with her letter after her death. I will date the letter before the date of her death."

"Perhaps it would work. I should not accept the gown, you know. It is most shocking to accept such an expensive gift from a gentleman."

"But we are friends and conspirators in banishing boredom, are we not?"

"There is something else worrying me."

He stretched out his long legs and leaned back on one elbow and looked up into her face.

"Everything is worrying you this evening, my chuck. Go on."

Frederica told him of the story about Lord M. that her mother had read out of the newspaper. "So you see," she ended, "if by any chance our friendship should be discovered, I should be well and truly in the suds. No one would believe the innocence of our friendship."

He laughed. "Then I would just need to marry you, my sweeting."

"Do not joke about a serious matter of this kind," she said bitterly. "A man such as you would never forgive me for allowing circumstances to force you to propose."

"I think if there had been even a murmur, a suspicion of our meetings, your papa would have immediately let you know in no uncertain terms."

"Yes, that is true. But every time we meet now, I will feel eyes all about us."

"There might be a compromise."

"Such as?"

The moonlight was shining on the cascade of her hair. She was hatless.

He touched a strand of her silky hair. "Do you never wear it up?"

"I shall surely be allowed to wear it up for the ball." She wound her tresses in one hand and swept her hair on top of her head and smiled at him.

He felt a tug at his heart and a feeling of danger but stubbornly refused to examine his feelings.

"So what is your compromise?" she asked.

"Instead of me having to walk such a way and skirt the village in order to see you, you could come to the grounds of Townley Hall."

"What of the gamekeepers? The lodge keeper?"

"I thought of them. There is a gazebo. . . ."

"But that is on the lawns and in full view of the hall!"

"No, not that one. There is a ruined one over near the west wall."

"Oh, I know the one," said Frederica. "And there is a break in the wall just about there. It would be easy for me to check that no one was about on the road, and the old gazebo is now surrounded by shrubbery."

An uncomfortable silence fell between them. Frederica felt she was treading farther into uncharted waters, and Lord Granton was wondering why he was about to pursue this odd and unsuitable friendship. After a few moments he scooped up the ball gown and left.

Chapter Four

Mrs. Hadley was shocked when the ball gown arrived for Frederica on the following day. She assumed that some carrier must have left it on the doorstep. All her daughters crowded around her as she read the letter aloud. Although the letter was addressed to Frederica, her mother had no compunction about opening it herself.

"Good heavens!" she exclaimed. "Old Lady Prebend is sending a ball gown to Frederica. I have not seen her in ages, and I was sure she did not know of Frederica's existence. See, it is only a short letter and dated back in the spring! How odd!"

She took out the gown and held it up. "It is really very fine."

"How kind of her," said Frederica. "I look forward to wearing it."

"Take it to your room," said her mother, coloring up. "I said, take it!" she snapped angrily.

After Frederica had gone, Mrs. Hadley went in search of her husband and finally found him in the church. She told him of the amazing gift and then wailed, "This is worse and worse. Frederica does not know she is not invited."

"I think we must tell her, my dear," said Dr. Hadley.

"But what if, in her disappointment, she does or says anything rude. Then we shall all be forbidden to go. It would break my poor girls' hearts."

"It might break Frederica's heart."

"Oh, tish! When has our Frederica shown herself in any way concerned over feminine things? She wanders the countryside, mooning about, or sits reading all day long."

"Perhaps," said Dr. Hadley, "if I were to call on Lady Crown and explain that Frederica is truly penitent and quite reformed, my lady might relent."

His wife looked at him doubtfully. "If you are sure it will not put her in a passion."

"I will try."

Dr. Hadley drove over to Townley Hall after changing into his best suit of clericals. He was ushered into the drawing room where Lady Crown and Annabelle were studying the latest fashion magazines.

"Dr. Hadley." Lady Crown smiled graciously. "You look very hot. May I offer you some lemonade?"

"Thank you, my lady. That would be most welcome."

Lady Crown rang the bell and told a footman to bring a jug of iced lemonade.

"I am gratified to hear you still have ice," said the rector.

"There is very little left in the icehouse," said Lady Crown. "This fierce weather."

"I am called," said the rector hesitantly, "to broach the subject of Frederica."

"Oh, that funny little girl," said Annabelle. "What has she done now?"

"Oh, nothing, nothing, and she is truly penitent for the distress she has caused you by her odd idea of humor. I wondered if you could be so gracious, so condescending as to consider allowing her to come to your ball. I have always been an admirer, my lady, of your great good nature, your Christian charity."

"Well . . . ," began Lady Crown, but Annabelle, with the memory still sharp in her mind of the way Lord Granton had paid all that unwelcome attention to Frederica, interrupted sharply, "No, I do not think so, Rector. Frederica has behaved shamefully and must be punished. Were she allowed to go to the ball after all, then she would feel free to behave in such a rude and thoughtless way again. She does not know the behavior that is due to her betters and must be taught a lesson."

The footman came in with the iced lemonade.

"Take it away, John," said Annabelle haughtily. "Dr. Hadley is just leaving."

Red in the face with heat and embarrassment, the rector bowed his way out.

When he related to his wife what had happened, she raised her hands in horror. "It is all Frederica's fault," she complained. "I should never have let you plead with them. We will take Frederica to one of the assemblies in Evesham in the autumn, but she must be content to stay at home on the night of the ball."

Upstairs in her room with the book of dancing steps in her hand, Frederica hummed to herself as she practiced. The splendid ball gown lay on the bed. Life was suddenly full of color and magic, and she would see him that night.

By evening tempers in the rectory were running high. The air was so still, so sticky, and so humid that everyone's nerves felt frayed. Mary was sulking over that ball gown, claiming it was much too fine for the youngest sister and that old Lady Prebend had muddled the names and had really meant it for her. Amy pointed out waspishly that Mary was too fat to wear it anyway. Frederica slipped upstairs and locked the ball gown in a chest in her room, suddenly afraid that one of her sisters would claim it as her own.

Amy said Harriet would never get any partners at the ball because her manner was too forward and her looks too blowsy. Harriet threw her fan at her sister. The fan struck Amy on the cheek, the ivory sticks leaving an angry red mark. Amy fell on Harriet and began to tug her hair, and both girls tumbled to the floor, clawing and shouting. Frederica heard the row as she slipped out of the back door, heard the angry voices fading behind her as she moved like a ghost through the still, heavy air.

As she was approaching the old gazebo, she heard away in the distance a rumble of thunder.

She looked uneasily up at the sky. But the moon shone clearly and the stars glittered.

The gazebo, unlike the splendid stone one nearer the house, was made of wood, now rotting and covered in creepers. Frederica wondered what it had been originally supposed to gaze upon, being so near the boundary wall. She stood outside, not liking the musty darkness of the interior, and waited anxiously, hearing the growling thunder draw ever nearer as if some great beast were stalking the countryside.

Lord Granton sat over his port and fretted. Sir Giles had said he had something of great import to discuss with him and so had delayed his leaving the dinner table. It transpired that Sir Giles wanted to ask his advice over a boundary dispute. He began to outline the details of what had happened. "It is Squire Huxtable's land, you see, and I showed him the maps, but he claims the maps were drawn up on the instructions of my father and were wrong. I do not want to take my neighbor to court, but what am I to do?" He then went on to describe at great length the various arguments he had had with the squire over the years.

At last Lord Granton interrupted impatiently by asking, "Just how much land is involved?"

"Three feet."

"Three feet!" exclaimed Lord Granton angrily. He swallowed the last of his port and got up. "You have asked my advice and it is this. Were it three feet of my land in question, I would gladly surrender it rather than be involved in a tedious and petty quarrel with one of my neighbors. Now if you will excuse me, I must return to my manuscript."

"I must say," complained Sir Giles huffily to the major, "that your friend seems to have little understanding of what is due to my position. Squire Huxtable is my social inferior and therefore should bend to *me*."

Lord Granton tore off his evening dress and put on a shirt and breeches, top boots and black coat and then made his escape. He heard the approaching storm and quickened his pace. He hoped Frederica had not waited for him. But as soon as he approached the gazebo, he saw the white glimmer of her gown in the darkness.

"This was not a very good idea," whispered Frederica. "This place is so old and dirty, and it looks about to fall down any moment. The boards on the floor inside are full of great holes, and there is nowhere for us to dance."

"We must forego our dancing and conversation tonight," he said hurriedly. "A storm is about to break. Come, I will walk you home."

"What if we are seen?"

"Everyone will be indoors. Come."

He helped her over the wall, and they walked together down the road. A great flash of lightning suddenly blinded them and Frederica cried out. He put an arm around her shoulders and hurried her forward. And then the heavens opened and the rain came down in sheets. As they approached the village, they saw candlelight flickering at the windows behind the thick cottage glass so that the flames looked like yellow smears.

"We will need to go round the village," shouted Frederica above the tumult of the storm.

He nodded and they both climbed over a stile and began to squelch across the fields. Frederica's thin gown was plastered to her body.

He now had his arm about her waist, urging her forward, reflecting that it was like crossing a battlefield. The storm was so great that the very ground seemed to heave in front of them.

They reached the back garden of the rectory. Frederica opened a gate in the high brick wall and they both entered, looking nervously up at the old house in case anyone was watching.

At the back door, her door as she thought of it, she whispered urgently, "Come up to my room until the storm has passed. You cannot possibly return in this weather."

It seemed logical not to stand arguing with her in the storm, or so he told himself. He followed her up the narrow stone staircase, wondering as he did so what excuse he would give if he found the rector waiting at the top.

But they were soon in her room with no one having seen them. Frederica locked them in and then went to a press in the corner and took out a large towel. "Try to dry yourself a little," she urged.

She took a towel out for herself, found dry clothes, and went behind the shelter of the bed curtains to change. When she emerged, he had stripped down to his waist and was scrubbing a very muscular chest. Her heart began to hammer against her ribs, and she remembered the story of Miss Bentley. She had lit two candles, and by their wavering light she saw nothing of the lover in Lord Granton's eyes, only a sort of devilish amusement.

"What a shocking pair we are," he murmured.

"It is as well the storm is so noisy," said Frederica. "Normally you can hear anything anyone says in this house."

He sat in a chair by the window after having wrung out his shirt over the basin on the toilet table and put it on. "I might leave my coat here," he said. "It is surely ruined."

"You had best take it with you," replied Frederica, "or I will have a difficult job getting rid of it."

He looked about him. "So this is your sanctuary." Candlelight fell on piles of books. Apart from the four-poster bed and two presses against the wall, there was a little table, the chair on which he was sitting, and a clutter of sewing material and fans and bits of inexpensive jewelry lying about the place. The ceiling was low and beamed.

"I have decided to leave the day after the ball," he said.

Suddenly Frederica's heart felt heavy and her

mind wrestled with the dismal vision of the empty days that lay ahead.

"I shall miss you," she said quietly.

"I shall write to you."

She shook her head. "That would not answer. Mama reads my letters."

"If I were as wicked as my reputation, I would ask you to run away with me."

Frederica's eyes were wide and startled. "As your mistress?"

"As my friend."

"Nothing so wicked there. Take me with you."

"If only I could, Frederica. But your reputation would be ruined beyond repair. You will soon meet a man you can love and marry. Listen, the storm is passing over. I must be on my way."

"I will show you out."

Frederica went and opened the door. Then she shrank back against him. "Wait!"

Mrs. Hadley's voice sounded clearly along the corridor. "I do declare this ball is causing more fuss and misery than I ever envisioned." Then there was the slamming of a door.

Frederica's body was pressed back against his own as they both listened to make sure no one else was about. He had an urge to turn her about, to hold her in his arms, and to kiss those soft virginal lips. Instead he gave her an impatient little push. "Lead the way, miss. We cannot stand here all night."

She led him quietly down the narrow staircase. The thunder rumbled away in the distance.

Something told him that he should not see her again, but he found himself saying, "Tomorrow night?"

"Not the gazebo," said Frederica.

"Then we will go back to the pool. If that poacher is around, he will not betray us."

"Till then."

He turned and walked away. He had not kissed her hand. Frederica sadly watched him go, heard the faint creak of the iron gate, and then there was only the great silence of the rain-washed night. She went slowly up the stairs. She would try not to think of the fact that he would be leaving for London so very soon now. She had another evening with him to look forward to. She would try so very hard not to think beyond that.

Lord Granton strode in the direction of the Hall. Moonlight was shining in the puddles and silvering the trees. Some night bird above his head chirped sleepily.

His conscience was beginning to nag him. Had he run mad going up to her room? What if they had been discovered?

In the morning Frederica rose very early and taking a basket of cordials and medicines went out to visit various sick parishioners. The day was fresh and fine. The air was full of the smells of bushes and flowers. She skipped over the puddles on the roads, singing under her breath, thinking only of the evening to come.

After she had done her rounds, she made her way back to the rectory — to find it in an uproar.

"What's amiss?" asked Frederica. Mrs. Hadley was stretched out on the sofa in the parlor having burned feathers held under her nose to revive her.

Amy and Harriet were clutching each other and emitting little shrieks.

"Papa is rounding up the men," said Mary. "We were nearly killed in our beds."

"Wh-when? H-how?" stammered Frederica.

"Mrs. Andrews, the baker's wife, said she saw a tall, villainous man creeping out of the rectory garden yesterday evening, just after the storm abated."

Frederica forced herself to look calm. "Did she see his face?"

"Yes, she said it was the face of evil, glittering eyes and a great scar down his cheek."

The great scar down Lord Granton's cheek had been caused by the effect of a branch casting a shadow across it in the moonlight.

Frederica let out a slow sigh of relief. "There is certainly no one of that description about. Perhaps it was just some tramp."

"We could all have been killed in our beds. I am going to write a poem about it," said Mary. "Some of the village men have volunteered to guard the rectory tonight."

Oh no, thought Frederica. I will not be able

to meet him, and I cannot even get a message to him!

"I shall never be suited to country life," grumbled Lord Granton to the major over a game of billiards.

"I find it very pleasant. We cannot be roistering every minute of the day."

"The pattern is the same. We eat a huge breakfast and walk with Annabelle and her mother and prattle, prattle, prattle. Then Sir Giles takes us on a drive to look at that wretched little piece of boundary that is in dispute, and we stand awkwardly while he trades insults with the squire. Then back to the Hall for nuncheon after which everyone stares at one another in glazed boredom. If we can avoid another expedition, then we hide away until the dressing bell sounds and so to dinner and then to Annabelle's harp. Perhaps we might even play cards for pennies."

"I find it all delightful," protested the major. "If I could watch Miss Annabelle play the harp for the rest of my days, I should consider myself the happiest of men."

"Then do not wait any longer. Propose to her. They cannot still believe I mean to drop the handkerchief."

"I am afraid they do. I am also afraid it is my fault."

"How so?"

"When you were so rude to Annabelle the last time we were over at the Blackstones', I felt I had to comfort her. I said something to the effect that your crusty manners were due to your nervousness over being about to enter the marital state for the first time."

Lord Granton carefully put down the billiard cue he had been holding and looked at his friend. "Then I suggest you undo the damage you have done. Can you not see what humiliation and misery you are building up for the girl? There we will all be at the ball with the Crowns waiting minute by minute for me to say something. They will probably put it about that my announcement is to be the highlight of the ball. Nothing happens. I take my leave the following day. Have you not thought of that? If you love Annabelle as much as you say you do, then it is your duty, man, to disabuse her and as soon as possible."

"I'll do it now," said the major miserably. He put on his coat and went in search of Annabelle. He found her in the sitting room with her mother.

"It is such a fine day," began the major, affecting a bluff cheerfulness he was far from feeling. "Would you care to walk with me for a little, Miss Annabelle?"

"Where is Lord Granton?"

"I do not know," lied the major.

"Oh, very well," she said, pouting. "I will fetch my bonnet."

The major struggled to make conversation with Lady Crown while he waited . . . and waited. A walk just outside meant a complete change of clothes for Annabelle. In fact, so much time was taken up each day changing in and out of gowns that she had little time to suffer any of the boredom that plagued Lord Granton.

At last she appeared, looking bandbox fresh, pretty, and quite sulky, for she had asked the servants to find Lord Granton and ask him to accompany them on their walk, and a footman had returned with the message that Lord Granton was working on his book.

As soon as they were in the privacy of the old rose garden, the major cleared his throat and said awkwardly, "I fear my friend, Lord Granton, has no intention of marrying anyone. If I have said anything that might have led you to think otherwise, then please forgive me."

Annabelle stopped short and stared at him. "I am sure you are mistaken. His very visit here is tantamount to a proposal."

"I am afraid Rupert only came here on a whim. I am very fond of him, but he is untrustworthy where the ladies are concerned."

Annabelle raised a handkerchief to her eyes. "But he must propose," she said. "Everyone expects him to!"

The major dropped to one knee on the path beside her.

He grasped the hand that was not holding the handkerchief and cried, "Oh, Miss Annabelle, I love you so. Be mine!"

She pulled her hand away. "What is this, Major Delisle?" She lowered the handkerchief. Her eyes were dry, and angry.

"I have loved you since I first set eyes on you," said the poor major.

The anger suddenly left Annabelle's eyes, and a smile began to curve her lips. "Do get to your feet, Major. We will forget this scene ever happened."

The major struggled up. "I will return to the house," said Annabelle, "and leave you to compose yourself. Oh, you *wicked* man!"

Annabelle went straight to her mother. "You will never believe what has happened! Major Delisle has just told me that Lord Granton does not mean to propose marriage to me."

"Oh dear," mourned Lady Crown. "I had begun to think that was indeed the case."

"Ah, but just listen. The good major proposed to me himself. Don't you see? He is trying to steal a march on his friend!"

Her mother looked at her doubtfully. "Annabelle, my love, are you sure?"

Annabelle laughed happily. She felt all-powerful, a breaker of men's hearts. The glory of the first proposal of marriage she had ever had seemed to surge through her veins.

"Trust me, Mama. I know the gentlemen."

Lady Crown was a doting mother, but she had an uneasy thought that this knowledge of men that her daughter claimed to have had not enticed one of that breed during the Season.

The major found Lord Granton in his room.

He was sitting in a chair by the window, reading. "How did it go?" asked the viscount, putting down his book.

"Good for you. Bad for me." The major pulled up a chair and sat opposite him. "I told her that you had no intention of proposing marriage. I proposed to her myself. She refused me. She not only refused me, worse than that. My proposal seemed to amuse her."

"The deuce it did!"

"But at least you should have no more worries."

"I am sorry you were rebuffed," said Lord Granton. "The Crowns must be furious with me. I will be especially pleasant at dinner tonight."

And so he was, and to such good effect that Annabelle glowed and kept flashing triumphant little see-I-told-you-so looks at her mother.

So well did Lord Granton behave that when he said he really must retire and get on with his writing, Sir Giles smiled and clapped him on the shoulder and said, "Musn't keep you from that, hey, m'boy?"

Lord Granton frowned at the familiarity of the gesture and the words, not knowing that Sir Giles already saw him as a son-in-law.

He went up to his room and quickly changed. Soon he was waiting by the pool. The night was still and quiet. The great heat had gone and everything smelled fresh and new. He waited and waited, wondering what had happened to her. He moodily threw a stone into the pool and watched the ripples spread. Had his visit to her room been discovered? He must have been mad.

After an hour he rose to his feet and made his way slowly back to the Hall. Frederica was only a little girl, barely out of the schoolroom. But she amused him and he so desperately wanted to be amused.

Frederica sat by her window and watched the village men patrolling the rectory garden. There was no way she could escape and get to that pool without being seen. He would think she had not troubled, could not be bothered. Perhaps they might have heard up at the Hall about the villainous stranger. But would they tell the viscount? And even if they did, would he expect the rectory to be so guarded that she could not get out? She waited and waited. At last about midnight she heard her father call out from the garden, "I think you can go home now, lads. I do not think we will be troubled again and you need your sleep."

Frederica still waited, hearing the men's voices as they said good night, seeing the lanterns bob away across the garden.

She seemed possessed of a madness. She had to see him, had to tell him why she had not come.

Without pausing to let one rational thought enter her brain, she swung a dark wool cloak about her shoulders, put a black felt bonnet on her head, which she usually wore only for village funerals, and crept down the back stairs and out into the silence of the night. She did not stop to think that there was no way she could see him, no way she could get into Townley Hall. She did not even know which room had been allocated to him.

She slid past the lodge and up the drive, keeping always to the shadow of the trees at the side. Only when the great bulk of the Hall came into view did she realize the folly of what she was doing. If she was surprised by one of the Hall gamekeepers, what excuse could she give?

Lord Granton put down the book he had been reading with a little sigh. He stood up and stretched and looked out of the window. He was about to turn away when a flicker of movement caught his eye. He raised the window and leaned out. He could swear there was a little figure over by the trees.

Could it be Frederica? Suddenly anxious, he swung himself over the sill and down the creeper outside and made for the trees.

"Rupert," said a little voice from the blackness.

"Frederica?"

"Over here."

She emerged from behind a tree.

"You should not have come here," he said angrily. "Have you no thought for your reputation?"

She shrank back a little. "I only came to tell you that you were seen last night."

"What!"

"Oh, they do not know it was you, and one of the villagers described you as a villain with a great scar on your cheek. So Papa had men patrolling the rectory garden tonight and I could not escape."

This is ridiculous, he thought suddenly. What am I, Lord Granton, doing encouraging the attentions of this village miss? All his life he had been pursued. Why should such as Frederica be the exception?

"Go home," he said angrily. "This folly must stop and I am only sorry I was such a fool to encourage you in it."

She did not protest. She curtsied low and said, "Yes, my lord. I am sorry to have offended you. We shall not meet again."

She turned and hurried away.

He had an impulse to run after her, but he stayed where he was, his hands clenched.

Frederica hurried home. She did not cry. She was too angry for that. She *hated* him. How dare he speak to her thus? How dare he make her feel like a trollop? To hell with him! Her dream of dancing with him at the ball and making everyone jealous was a silly one. She would send that ball gown back to him, and she would tell her mother she had lost it.

But when she got back to her room and looked at that ball gown, she knew she could never have the heart to return anything quite so beautiful. She would never have another dress like it ever again.

Lord Granton awoke with a heavy, depressed feeling. At first he could not think why he felt so low, and then he remembered that bitter little scene with Frederica the night before. He should not have snapped at her like that. There was no one like Frederica. She had made the friendly gesture to try to let him know why she had been unable to meet him, and he had treated her like an importunate debutante.

He must find some way to see her, to convey his apologies to her. Like many aristocrats, Lord Granton had never bothered to analyze his motives from the day he was born. He did not want Frederica to think badly of him, and that was that. He had to see her. No one could possibly suspect him of romantic overtures to a young miss who still wore her hair down.

So when hailed by Sir Giles as he was leaving the breakfast table and asked where he was going, he said he had found the old church very interesting and had decided to have another look at it. The major stared at his friend in surprise, wondering at this sudden interest in old churches, and then remembered that odd little girl at the rectory.

"We will all go," said Sir Giles. "Annabelle quite dotes on churches."

And so Lord Granton had to wait and fume and fret while Annabelle went upstairs to consult her lady's maid about the best outfit to wear for viewing a church and to have her hair rearranged.

He was in a mood that the major privately thought of as surly when they finally set out.

They drove straight to the church. "Should we not call at the rectory and explain our presence?" suggested Lord Granton.

"No need for that," said Sir Giles heartily. "The church is always open."

"But there are a few questions I would like to ask Dr. Hadley," pursued Lord Granton.

"I am sure we will be able to answer any questions you might have," said Lady Crown.

To Lord Granton's relief Dr. Hadley bustled in only a few moments after their arrival with offers of refreshment at the rectory.

"I am sure we can entertain Lord Granton back at the Hall," said Lady Crown, and then found to her irritation that the viscount was already accepting the invitation.

Lord Granton, to keep up the fiction that he was really interested in the church, proceeded to ask a great many questions about it while Annabelle fretted, fidgeted, and yawned.

At last they walked over to the rectory. Mrs. Hadley had seen the carriage outside the church and had her daughters all arranged in the drawing room.

"We can stay only a short while," protested Lady Crown. "Lord Granton has a busy day."

"I cannot think of anything," said Lord Granton. He smiled at Frederica, but that young lady was studying the toes of her shoes as if they were the most fascinating things she had ever seen.

"We had a great scare here, my lord," said Mary. "Some villain was seen lurking about the rectory, and the villagers patrolled the grounds. He must have been some passing footpad. But only think, we could all have been murdered in our beds!"

"Were you frightened, Miss Frederica?" asked Lord Granton.

There was a silence, and everyone looked at Frederica, and Frederica looked at her shoes.

"Lord Granton has just asked you a question, miss," snapped Lady Crown.

Frederica raised her head. "What was the question?" she asked. "I was thinking of something else."

Lord Granton looked amused and everyone else, irritated.

"I asked if you were frightened, Miss Frederica," he said.

"Last night was something I would rather not think about," replied Frederica. "When unpleasant things happen, my lord, I put them out of my mind and go on as if they had never really happened."

"I am working on a poem of the event," said Mary eagerly. "I have the first stanzas."

"Spare us," said Annabelle faintly. "It is too fine a day to listen to poetry."

Tea was served. Lady Crown hoped Lord Granton would refuse, but he not only accepted tea but two scones as well, which he proceeded to eat with maddening slowness.

"Are you all looking forward to the ball?" asked Lord Granton.

"Very much," said Amy, casting him a flirtatious look.

"We have been practicing our steps," put in Harriet.

"And you, Miss Frederica, have you been practicing your steps?"

"But . . . ," began Lady Crown.

"Frederica cannot dance," said Mrs. Hadley firmly, not wanting the Crowns to tell Frederica that she was not invited.

"Have you nothing to say for yourself, Miss Frederica?" Lord Granton looked steadily at Frederica and Frederica looked steadily back.

"No," she said bluntly.

There was a shocked little silence. Lord Granton felt like tearing his hair out. But he leaned back in his chair, the picture of elegance, and smiled at Frederica.

"I am sure your sisters will be able to help you. Every young lady should know how to dance."

Annabelle looked from one to the other with narrowed eyes. "That is the problem of holding a ball in the country," she said. "So many people do not know how to dance properly."

"Has that been your experience, Miss Frederica?"

Frederica looked at Lord Granton with hurt and angry eyes. "As I do not dance, my lord, I have had little opportunity of finding out whether people perform well or not."

"But you must have observed them."

A little flash of malice lit up Frederica's fine eyes. "My lord, I have no accomplishments. Amy, on the other hand, is a very fine artist. You must see her watercolors."

Gratified, Amy rose to her feet and went to collect her portfolio, which she had placed ready behind the sofa.

Minx, thought Lord Granton as he took out his quizzing glass and studied one inferior painting after another.

"And Harriet is an accomplished pianist," said Frederica when Lord Granton had come to the end of the watercolors.

Harriet rushed to the pianoforte. She played competently, but very loudly and with little feeling for the music. It was a very long piece. It went on and on. Lord Granton looked at Frederica, but she was once more looking at her shoes. That chit is going to forgive me, he thought. He slid his quizzing glass down into the cushions at the back of his chair.

Lady Crown felt she had endured enough. She got to her feet.

"We really must go," she shouted above the noise of Harriet's chords.

Mrs. Hadley fussed about them as they went outside. She wanted to apologize for Frederica's rudeness but did not want to call further attention to it.

"Thank goodness that is over," said Annabelle

as they drove off. "What a monstrous bore. And that Frederica! So farouche. She must really have given you a disgust of her, Lord Granton."

"Good heavens, I have left my quizzing glass. Stop the carriage," called Lord Granton to the coachman.

"But we can send a servant to collect it," protested Sir Giles.

The carriage stopped and Lord Granton jumped out onto the road. "I feel like walking," he called.

"So do I," said Annabelle. "Wait! I will come with you." But when she climbed down, it was to find that he was already some way off down the road and hurrying away.

Frederica was getting a resounding lecture from her family on her bad behavior when Lord Granton was announced. They broke off their tirade and stared at him, openmouthed.

"I left my quizzing glass," he said, bowing all round.

Frederica went straight to the chair in which he had been sitting, put her hand down the cushions, and then produced the quizzing glass. She curtsied to him as she handed it over.

"Some more tea?" said Mrs. Hadley.

"You are very kind." He sat down. He was determined to stay until he had managed to convey to Frederica that he was sorry for what he had said.

"Delighted to have your company," beamed Mrs. Hadley. "Where is that maid? Excuse me, my lord. Frederica, come with me."

Frederica followed her mother from the room.

"Go upstairs and stay there," hissed her mother furiously. "I will speak to you later." She bit her lip. Why could she not find the courage to tell this youngest daughter of hers that she could not go to the ball?

Frederica went upstairs and sat by the window. She had seen him hide that quizzing glass. Her heart beat hard. Had he come back to try to have a word with her? She heaved a little sigh. She would never know now.

Downstairs, Lord Granton clutched a teacup and listened to one of Mary's longest poems. When at last it was finished, he asked, "Where is Miss Frederica?"

"She is abovestairs, I believe," said Mrs. Hadley. "You must excuse her behavior. Frederica is not used to company."

"Not surprising," he said dryly, "as she obviously has not been in the way of enjoying any mannered society or being gowned to suit her position."

"She is very young," said Mrs. Hadley, coloring up.

"She is eighteen and should be wearing her hair up. She should also be able to dance."

"My lord, you obviously do not understand the difficulties in having four daughters to bring up."

"Obviously not." He put down his teacup. "Now I really must be on my way."

In vain did they press him to stay. He strode

off in a foul mood. Be damned to the girl. He was making a cake of himself over the chit.

But when he was outside the garden, he found himself walking around to the lane that led along the back of the vicarage. He stood irresolutely by the gate and looked up. Frederica was sitting by the window. He let himself into the garden. Her window was open.

"I did not mean it," he called up. "Not a word. I was worried about you. Please meet me tonight."

She looked steadily down at him and then gave a little nod.

"Lord Granton!"

He swung round. Dr. Hadley was approaching round the side of the house.

"I was admiring your garden," said Lord Granton. Above his head he heard the window close.

"Indeed!" Dr. Hadley looked around in a bewildered way at a rather dreary expanse of scrubby grass and shrubs. "You must be funning, my lord. The gardens at the back of the rectory are unkempt, to say the least."

"That is just what attracts me," said Lord Granton earnestly. "I detest formal gardens. I like a wilderness."

"You certainly have it here," commented the rector.

"I must be on my way, Dr. Hadley. Thank you for showing me your gardens." He strode off. Dr. Hadley watched him go, a puzzled frown on his face.

Lord Granton felt relieved and cheerful. He would see her that night. Somewhere a little voice was trying to tell him that his behavior was outrageous but he ignored it. The day was fine and sunny and everything was all right with the world.

That was until he got back to Townley Hall. He had made no mental note of the social engagements his hosts had arranged for him and so was surprised that evening to find his valet laying out his best evening clothes.

"What is this, Gustave? Too fine for a family dinner."

"It is the Blackstones' ball this evening."

"I cannot go!"

The major came in just in time to hear the last words. "Rupert, you must. If you do not go, they will be disappointed and angry. A great number of people have accepted the Blackstones' invitation with a view to meeting you."

Lord Granton scowled furiously, but he could see no way out of his dilemma. He did not trust servants to be discreet, any servants, even Gustave. Gustave would certainly find a way to deliver a note to Frederica, but then Gustave was always in love with some housemaid or other, and he would gossip, and the gossip might spread. Jack Muir, the poacher, was to be trusted, only because he might find himself dangling on the end of a rope if he opened his mouth about it.

At last, feeling like a prisoner, he set out with the Crowns and the major for the Blackstones' ball. She would wait by that pool, and he would not come, and that would be that.

His temper was so bad that he decided to fight it and behave as well as possible. This he did to such good effect that Annabelle glowed with triumph and all the Blackstones' guests said that his reputation must have been all a hum, for he did not appear wicked at all. He even danced with several of the wallflowers.

Frederica sat by the pool and waited. At first she could not really believe that he would not come. But as a whole hour passed, she realized that something must have happened. She had a sudden vision of what her life would be after he had gone. For some nights she would probably come and sit here, waiting and always hoping to hear the sound of his step, just as she was doing tonight.

And then she heard someone approaching and sprang up, but the smile of welcome died on her face as she recognized the figure of the poacher.

"Are you spying on me?" she asked angrily.

He touched his greasy hat. "No, miss. I was keeping clear, like."

"Then what do you want with me?"

"You don't think that Lord Granton will report having seen me in these here woods to Sir Giles?"

"I do not think so, Jack. He would have to explain what he was doing here himself."

Frederica, unlike her parents and the Crowns but like a good many of the villagers, knew of

Jack's poaching activities. "You will be caught one day, Jack," she said, "and you know the penalties are severe."

"You are very young, miss."

"What's that to do with anything?"

"Just that when a great lord meets a young girl on the sly, reckon it don't bode no good for the girl."

"We are friends, that is all, and you are being impertinent."

"S'pose it's your business, miss, and no one will hear a word from me. He won't be coming anyhows."

"Why is that?"

"Blackstones are having a big ball tonight. Look, miss, there is even talk that he'll announce his engagement to Miss Annabelle this night without waiting for the ball at the Hall."

"Oh," said Frederica in a little voice.

"So you see, miss, it don't seem right to me that he should be sneaking off to meet you while courting t'other. I mean, it looks like he don't reckon you good enough."

"Off with you, Jack. You are talking about things of which you know nothing."

He touched his cap again. "Have a heed, Miss Frederica." Then he backed silently off into the blackness of the woods.

Frederica sat down slowly again by the pool. She found her hands were shaking and clasped them tightly together. All her innocent dreams were crashing about her ears. How could she have been so naive? She did not think his motives in meeting her base. She was sure that he was only amusing himself.

But the fact that he was really courting Annabelle gave her turbulent emotions. She had imagined he would marry one day, perhaps soon, and her mother would read the announcement of the betrothal in the social columns. Her magic picture of dancing with him at the ball in her new gown now seemed childish. She would need to stand at that ball and listen to Sir Giles announce his engagement to Annabelle — that was unless the announcement was being made even at this very moment.

He was in a world from which she was barred because of her age, because she was the youngest daughter, because of her inferior social position. She did not belong to his world and never could.

A little breeze rustled the leaves above her head, and she shivered and got to her feet. Time to put childish dreams away. Time to lose herself in books again and stop inventing fictional stories in real life.

She had just gained the security of her room and was preparing for bed when her mother came in. Frederica swung round, startled. She could not remember the last time her mother had visited her room.

"Where have you been?" demanded Mrs. Hadley. "I called earlier."

"I felt restless," said Frederica, "and walked over to the church."

Mrs. Hadley sat down on the bed and took a deep breath. "You have never troubled yourself much over frivolities, Frederica, and considering your rude behavior to the Crowns today, do you not think it would be better if you did not attend the ball?"

Frederica looked at her wide-eyed. "I have not troubled myself over frivolities, as you put it, Mama, in the past, for the simple reason I have not been allowed to do so. I am determined to attend the ball, and furthermore I am going to wear my hair up."

"But your behavior to the Crowns . . ."

"I have apologized for that, Mama. They irritate me with their contempt, their condescending airs. I feel they need a good set-down."

There was iron in Frederica's voice and Mrs. Hadley shuddered. She had come to get the painful business of telling Frederica that she was not to attend the ball over and done with.

But now she decided it would not answer. What if the Crowns called again and a disappointed Frederica was even ruder than ever? Then all invitations would be canceled.

"Very well," she said crossly. "But do not blame me if you find the Crowns have taken you in dislike. You must learn to be more civil to your betters, Frederica."

"I consider the Crowns my inferiors."

"How dare you! The next time they call, if they call, keep to your room."

"Gladly," said Frederica.

Mrs. Hadley went out and slammed the door behind her.

Frederica felt miserable. Her mother had the right of it. Being nasty to the Crowns was dangerous. Dr. Hadley owed his living to them. Perhaps it would be better if she did not attend that ball. But, oh, that beautiful gown. She *must* go.

Chapter Five

Lord Granton awoke feeling more like a prisoner under house arrest than ever. The weather had turned warm and sultry again. He decided to go without breakfast, to walk toward the village. Perhaps he might by chance come across Frederica.

But there seemed to be a great many people moving about as he walked in the direction of the village, and he realized he could hardly walk about unnoticed. The news that he was abroad spread quickly to the rectory. The girls were told to put on their prettiest gowns, and Frederica was ordered to stay in her room.

Frederica decided to go to the stream and sit and watch the cool rushing water, for if Lord Granton called, she felt she could not bear to be shut up in her room on this fine day, hearing the sound of his voice belowstairs.

The pine wood was quiet and still. She walked through it, her feet making no sound on the carpet of needles at her feet.

She had taken a copy of the *Ladies' Magazine* to read. Usually she read only the more serious essays, but for the first time she found herself reading an account of the gowns worn at a royal party. In comparison to the dresses worn by the aristocracy in London, her ball gown began to seem like nothing out of the common way. The Countess of Grosvenor, she read, had been wearing a crepe petticoat embroidered with draperies and variegated silver cord, with a border at the bottom to correspond. The train was of sea green satin and her headdress of diamonds and ostrich feathers. And here was the Duchess of Rutland: dress entirely of lace, the petticoat of honiton lace over pink sarcenet, the two draperies of point lace intermixed with wreaths of roses and jessamine, the draperies looped up with two long chains of diamonds; pink silk train, trimmed with lace; girdle and stomacher of diamonds.

But, then, these were court dresses, and at Court the ladies still sometimes wore the paniered gowns of the last century, often so bedecked with jewels and ornaments, she had heard, that they could hardly move.

She sighed and turned the pages to more serious matters. Here was an essay outlining the difference between men and women. "Could women," she read, "be admitted to an equality with men, be recognised as rational partners, divide with them the schemes of life, enjoying the full intercourse of intellect, it certainly would be a beautiful scene; besides, the collision of so many developed understandings would undoubtedly contribute to the advancement of civilisation. We know not what revolutions in government might be saved, or to what sudden perfection laws might attain."

"So this is where I find you!"

She gave a little gasp and looked up. Lord Granton smiled down at her.

Frederica put down her magazine and stood up. "Are you sure you have not been seen?" she asked anxiously. "The rectory was abuzz with the news of your approach, and I was sent to my room."

"Why?" he demanded sharply.

"Mama is afraid I might be rude, and she has the right of it. I am truly badly behaved."

"I took care not to be seen," he remarked. Frederica looked at him doubtfully. "I should think it is very hard for a gentleman, six feet tall, and dressed in the height of Bond Street fashion to pass anywhere in the countryside on a sunny day unnoticed."

"I may have been seen coming here, but what matter? No one knows you are here. Now, I was caught last night with the Blackstones' ball."

"So I heard."

"Ah, so you did not expect me?"

"It was Jack Muir who told me. I went to the pool. How did you guess I would be here this morning and not at the pool?"

"Because here is nearer to the rectory. What are you reading?" He took the magazine from her.

"This piece." She pointed to the bit she had just read.

He smiled and said, "You should have read on. It goes on to say, 'The idea of exalting man above the whole creation, without exception and without an equal, is very grand and noble, nor can it be thought much degradation to a woman to obey so distinguished a lord.' "

"Why cannot I believe that?" said Frederica.

"Ah and here is a lovely piece. 'If a man stretches out his arm to a woman and woman leans upon his bosom, the picture is found in every heart in the world.' "

"Let us sit down," said Frederica sharply, "and talk of something else."

She sat down and glared at the rushing water, her back ramrod straight.

He lounged beside her. "So what shall we talk about? Although I could argue it was a very womanly trait to abandon the subject when you are losing the argument."

"Did you propose to Annabelle Crown last night?"

"No, I did not. Nor do I think it is expected of me."

"Are you sure? Papa says that your visit to the Crowns was always viewed as a proposal of marriage."

"Had I married every miss in every household I have stayed in over the years, I would be a sort of pasha by now."

"I think you are expected to, you know."

"The major has gone to great lengths on my behalf to disabuse them of that, and they still seem tolerably pleased with my company."

"If you say so. You have more experience in

matters of the heart than I."

"Really, Frederica, I should say you had no experience in matters of the heart at all."

"That is because of my age. I will learn."

"Aha. So this independent young miss who dares to doubt the superiority of men plans to have affairs of the heart?"

"It is not beyond the bounds of possibility." Frederica laughed. "With such a ball gown, I feel I could actually break hearts."

There was a rather heavy silence. Lord Granton was thinking that he had vaguely thought Frederica would always remain the same, always virginal, always waiting in the Cotswolds for him should he decide to return.

"It would mean giving up your independence," he said at last.

"What independence? I have begun to think of marriage in a different light. Look at my present circumstances. I am considered a child, wear hand-me-down gowns, and do not put my hair up. Were I married to some amiable man, I would have an establishment of my own. I would have children, perhaps a horse and a dog. I would be free."

"You would have to obey your husband."

"I said, amiable man. I have begun to study married men in the village. Some of them, it seems, have to obey their wives!"

"But since your parents have hitherto kept you back in a most unnatural way, how do you expect to meet a suitor?"

"There are various winter assemblies and now I can dance. You have been a great help to me, Rupert, because now, too, I will not only be able to dance but to converse."

"My dear Frederica, I do not think you should converse with any gentleman the way you converse with me. You will have to learn to flirt."

"Like my sisters?"

"I do not want to criticize your sisters, but I would suggest a little more finesse. Do you know how to flirt?"

"I think so."

"Very well. Miss Frederica, you enchant me."

"I cannot quite cope with that, Rupert. It seemed too bold, too warm a compliment."

"Perhaps. Try this. It is amazing how well our steps match, Miss Frederica."

She gave him a glinting sideways glance and lowered her long eyelashes. "Why, sir, that is because you are such an excellent dancer. Where you lead, I follow."

"What a little actress you are," he said somewhat crossly.

"But all ladies need to be actresses, do you not think?"

"I should have thought genuine regard and respect might enter into it somewhere."

"La, and I am considered the innocent! When in all your amours did you hold the lady in respect or regard?"

"Not until now."

"Rupert, behave yourself or we cannot be friends."

"Forgive me, but you take me too seriously. I, too, was practicing to flirt."

"I do not think you need any practice at all."

Frederica stared angrily down at the magazine that now lay on the grass beside her. The wind turned the pages. She suddenly stiffened. There in the poetry section was a poem titled "The Contented Soldier." The first line seemed to jump up at her: "I hear the raindrops patt'ring fast."

So Mary had not written that poem. She had merely copied it from this two-month-old edition of the *Ladies' Magazine*!

"What is it?" he asked. "I did not mean to offend you."

"Nothing," said Frederica, closing the magazine. She suddenly did not want to betray her sister's vanity.

She picked up the magazine and stood up. "I must go. I will be missed, I think, if I stay here much longer."

He stood up as well, towering over her, his tall figure blotting out the sun.

"So I will see you at the pool tonight?"

Frederica felt afraid. She should not go on seeing him in this underhanded way. If he were a proper gentleman, he would call on her parents and ask their permission to pay his addresses to her. And then she blushed at the folly of her thoughts. Such as Lord Granton would never,

ever consider her marriageable. And soon he would be gone, and she would be left with nothing but books and dreams.

"Very well," she said. He made to take her hand, but she slid nimbly past him and ran off through the wood, her white gown flickering in the shafts of sunlight striking through the trees.

Remember poor Miss Bentley, jeered a warning voice in her head. She lost her reputation for a reason. You are in danger of losing yours over nothing more than a friendship.

Lord Granton returned to the Hall to find everyone waiting impatiently for him. "Ah, there you are!" cried Sir Giles. "We were about to set off without you."

"Where are we going?" asked Lord Granton, fighting down a nagging feeling of boredom laced with irritation.

"It is such a warm day that we have decided to go on the river."

He had a longing to say he did not want to go on the river, that all he wanted to do was lounge around and read. But he forced a smile on his face and said it sounded like a pleasant idea.

He forced himself to converse with Annabelle and her mother as they were driven to the banks of the Avon where Sir Giles's barge was moored. As he sipped champagne and talked to Annabelle about what a splendid fellow the major was, and he could not understand why some lady had not snapped him up long before this, Lord Granton felt that old heavy cloud of boredom settling down on him. The barge slid its slow way along the Avon, a horse pulling it. A canopy to protect them from the sun fluttered over their heads. It was just about as exciting as the drawing room at the Hall, he thought. The only advantage was that Annabelle had not brought her harp. He then realized that he had not properly explained or apologized to Frederica for his rude behavior when she had called at the Hall. He would tell her that evening — if evening ever came. How long the day seemed!

Frederica is bored and I am bored, he thought. It is because of too much idleness, too much time to think. When this tedious visit is over, I shall return to my estates and interest myself in agriculture and stop trying to fill my days with social events, prize fights, dreary balls, and all the other curses of the social round. Time to settle down. But settling down meant a wife and children. Had he married younger, so his thoughts ran, he would have followed the pattern of finding a suitable wife with a suitable dowry. But now he wanted someone who would be a pleasant companion.

He roused himself from his reverie to say to Annabelle, who was leaning over the side of the barge, "Do not lean too far, Miss Annabelle, or you will fall over."

She turned a laughing face to him. "It is quite safe. I am looking for fish."

She turned back and that was when the branch

of a tree stretching over the water caught her and swept her overboard.

Lady Crown screamed and fainted. Lord Granton tore off his coat and boots and jumped over the side. He swam to where Annabelle had disappeared. Dimly he heard the major calling frantically to the man leading the horse that was pulling the barge to stop. Lord Granton dived, surfaced, and dived again. The second time his fingers grasped cloth, and he seized Annabelle round the waist and swam up, gasping with relief when his head broke the surface.

He swam to the bank where the bargee was waiting. Annabelle was pulled up and Lord Granton heaved himself onto the grassy bank after her. He stared down at her limp body and white face and then seized her arms and pumped them up and down as he had seen fishermen do once in trying to save the life of one of their friends. Water gushed from her mouth, and then she gave a faint groan and vomited up more water. The barge was now moored at the side, and Sir Giles came running toward them followed by the major.

Lord Granton rubbed Annabelle's wrists and in desperation slapped her face. She opened her eyes and began to cry.

"Oh, thank God," said Sir Giles, who began to cry as well, as did the major, while Lord Granton glared at them.

"Send your man for the carriage," he shouted. "The sooner we get her home and in bed and send for the physician, the better."

Rugs from the barge were fetched and Annabelle's body wrapped in them. Then the carriage arrived along the tow path, and she was lifted into it.

Back at the Hall, Sir Giles, the major, and Lord Granton paced up and down, waiting for the verdict of the physician who was abovestairs in Annabelle's bedchamber. At last he came down.

"She will do very well now," he said. "Thanks to your prompt rescue, my lord, you saved her life."

Sir Giles flung his arms around the embarrassed viscount, calling him a trojan, the best of men, proclaiming that God had sent him on this visit, that he would always be indebted to him, while the major dismally watched and wished with all his heart that he had been able to swim.

The news of the rescue spread quickly from the Hall servants to the village, and so the rectory got the news by early evening. "And it is said," declared Mrs. Hadley, "that Sir Giles believes this marriage-to-be was meant by God."

Frederica finally slipped away to her room. She felt very low. Lord Granton had saved a fair maiden from drowning, just like in a romance, except the fair maiden had not been Frederica. For the first time in her young life, Frederica felt bitterly and irrationally jealous. Annabelle had everything: looks, money, and now dramatic adventure.

The result was that when she set out for the pool later that evening, she half expected he would not come to visit such a nonentity as Frederica Hadley.

But he was already there, his face unreadable in the gloom.

"I heard about your heroism," said Frederica.

"Oh, that." They sat down together on the grass. "I never did apologize for my bearish behavior when I found you outside the Hall," he went on.

"Why were you so very angry with me?"

"I forgot your age, your innocence, and our friendship. You must realize I am used to being pursued by young ladies. I am truly sorry."

"You will soon be married, and young ladies will have no reason to pursue you any longer, Rupert."

"I have no immediate plans to marry."

"But the whole village is talking of your heroism. Marriage to Annabelle is viewed as inevitable. It is believed that Divine Providence sent you on this visit simply to rescue Annabelle and then wed her."

"It is amazing how many people see the workings of Divine Providence in just about everything. The silly girl leaned too far over the edge of the barge and got caught by the branch of a tree hanging over the river and was swept into the water. She is lucky to be alive."

"Reports say she was dead when you pulled her from the water, but you restored her to life."

"Your common sense should tell you that the dead cannot be restored to life, Frederica."

"Barton Sub Edge has not ever heard anything more romantic. You will have to marry her now."

"My sweeting, I will not be coerced into marriage."

"All I can say is that at that ball, the Crowns are going to be one very disappointed family."

And then some imp prompted him to say, "And would you be a very disappointed young lady if I did propose to Annabelle?"

Her face was a white glimmer in the darkness of the night. "Your amours are nothing to do with me," said Frederica.

"But as my friend, surely you have some views on the subject."

"Then, Rupert, may I say that I think you and Annabelle very well suited."

He found himself becoming angry. "And why is that?"

"Annabelle Crown is eminently suitable. She is pretty and complacent. She is used to living in a large household. She is a trifle young for you, but age does not seem to matter in a suitable marriage."

"You do not think I should marry for love?"

"Love, I think, is not just passion but involves respect and trust."

"You can hardly be qualified on the subject."

"I have my powers of observation. I do not need to be trained as a carpenter to know that a table is badly made."

"That comment is not original. You are paraphrasing Dr. Johnson."

"A worthy source." Frederica felt sour and, yes, lonely. The lightness of their friendship seemed to have gone. He had not offered to teach her any more dances, and she was now stubbornly determined not to ask him.

Silly little girl, thought Lord Granton.

But both sat side by side, neither moving.

Then he gave a reluctant laugh. "I do declare, my sweeting, we are having our first quarrel."

"Quarrels are for lovers."

"And for friends, too. If you continue to sit there in a bad temper, I will not teach you the waltz."

"Oh, would you do that? Would you really?" cried Frederica, leaping to her feet, all her bad temper forgotten.

He got up as well and held out his hand. "Come here. I put my hand at your waist so. Now I will sing the melody."

He began to hum, breaking off occasionally to say things like, "Let me lead. Follow me. Do not look at your feet."

She was conscious of the warmth of that hand at her waist. She half closed her eyes and followed his steps, seeming to drift dreamily over the grass.

He noticed she was wearing a light rose perfume, the scent of summer. He stopped at last and with a laugh wound a strand of her long silky hair around one finger.

"How will you manage to put your hair up? Will your sisters help you?"

"They will not need to. I have been studying articles on how to create one of the new Roman styles. Should I try to make one of the new Turkish turbans?"

"And eclipse the bright glory of your hair? No, what you need are little pearls threaded through it."

"I think Mama has some. Thank you. That is a fine idea. Now I really must go."

"I will go first and make sure no one is about, and then you follow." He released her hair and gave her a casual pat on the cheek and strode away.

Frederica watched him go. She felt sad, confused, elated, all mixed in together.

After ten minutes she made her way through the woods and across the field. She climbed over the stile and onto the road, and then stiffened. The figure of a woman was standing right in the middle of the road.

"Who's there?" demanded Frederica sharply.

"Beth Judge."

"Oh, Beth, you startled me." Beth Judge was a gnarled old woman who lived in one of the shabbier cottages at the end of the village. The children thought she was a witch.

"I seed you, miss," said Beth.

"Well, of course you did," said Frederica with a lightness she did not feel. "Here I am."

"I mean," said Beth, coming up close, so that

Frederica could smell the nasty odors of her old unwashed body, "I seed you with that there grand lord, a-dancing. What would the rector say?"

"You won't say anything!" cried Frederica.

"Reckon I can keep my mouth shut — for two guineas."

"Two guineas." Frederica looked at her in horror. She could not clearly see her face in the darkness, only the glitter of her malignant old eyes. "I have not got two guineas. Where on earth am I going to get a sum like that?"

"You'd better think o' something, missie. If I ain't got them two golden boys by noon tomorrow, the rector gets to hear of it."

Frederica took to her heels and ran past Beth. What on earth was she going to do? Lord Granton might know, but how could she reach him?

Frederica spent a sleepless night and awoke very early. And then she thought of an idea. She would go out to the henhouses and collect as many eggs as were there, put them in a basket, and take them up to Townley Hall. If her parents found out about it, she would simply say that she was in a way making amends for her bad behavior.

She dressed in her best, such as it was. Her new gowns had not yet been made up by the dressmaker. She collected a basket from the kitchen and went out to the henhouses, disturbing some still sleepy hens and collecting warm new eggs.

She set out for Townley Hall. The day was not yet too warm and was glorious in the sunlight. It should have been a day to be happy, not feeling guilty and frightened. She knew where her father kept his purse and could easily steal those two guineas, but somehow such an action seemed even more abhorrent than being found out.

The butler opened the door to her. Frederica explained the reason for her early visit. He held out his hand. "I will take these to the kitchen, Miss Frederica, but the ladies are still abed, Miss Annabelle recovering from her ordeal."

Frederica clutched the basket to her and looked up at him, wide-eyed. What a fool she was! She should have realized they would all still be asleep.

"I would like to present these to Lady Crown myself," she said firmly. "I will return later."

Lord Granton, descending the staircase in order to have an early breakfast before anyone else was awake, saw the little figure of Frederica confronting the butler.

He strode forward. "Good morning, Miss Frederica," he said. "Can I be of assistance?"

He saw the relief in her eyes. "I am come to deliver some new-laid eggs to the Hall, but, of course, the ladies are all still abed."

"Then leave them with Paxton here and let me walk you to the end of the drive."

Frederica handed over the basket of eggs and

walked slowly across the forecourt with Lord Granton until they were out of earshot, for the butler was still standing at the entrance, looking after them curiously.

"It is terrible, truly terrible," began Frederica. She told him about the blackmail by Beth Judge.

"Tell me about this Judge woman," he said, "and do not look so frightened. It is no use me giving you two guineas for her, for after I am gone, she will be back for more and will never give up."

"She is nasty and horrid and old," said Frederica. "When I was at school, we all thought she was a witch. She sells love potions and things like that and reads one's fortune in the tea leaves."

"Does she, now! Well, my chuck, tell me where she lives."

"It is the second cottage you reach as you approach the village. On the left-hand side of the road, a very tumbledown place."

"Leave the matter with me. Go home and forget about it."

"Rupert . . ."

"I said, go home. I will see you tonight."

She gave a little shiver despite the heat of the day. "It is no longer safe."

"Then there must be somewhere safer. What about the church?"

"But that is holy ground!"

"And we are not about to do anything unholy. Is it locked at night?"

"Papa never locks it. He says that there is always someone in need of a place of worship day or night."

"Sensible man. Until then."

She looked up at him doubtfully. "Run along, child," he said gently. "You have nothing to fear."

Frederica hurried away. As she reached the lodge, she turned and looked back. He was standing in the middle of the drive, watching her. He raised his hand in a salute and then spun on his heel and strode back to the Hall.

Beth Judge squinted at the battered old carriage clock she kept on the table in her parlor. Nearly noon. Frederica would come and Frederica would have that money. Beth smiled slowly. She liked the feeling of power that blackmail gave her.

There was a firm knock at the door. Already planning what she would do with those two guineas, she shuffled over, opened the door, and fell back apace.

Lord Granton was standing on her doorstep, his hat in his hand. For one shaky moment she thought he looked like the devil himself, but then she rallied. "Step into my parlor, my lord."

"Said the spider to the fly," he remarked dryly. He followed her in, put his hat, stick, and gloves on the table, and sat down.

"You have been threatening Miss Frederica Hadley and trying to get money out of her."

She grinned. "I don't reckon you want anyone to know about it either."

"Listen here," he said calmly, "and listen well. You have the reputation of being a witch, a reputation that has, shall I say, never been substantiated. Not until now."

She sat down in a rocking chair. "What d'you mean?"

"I mean if you ruin my reputation, I will ruin yours. I will say you deliberately set out to lure Miss Hadley and myself to that pool, that you were seen flying overhead on your broomstick."

Although the witches' gallows had been taken down in the seventeenth century and old village women no longer went in fear of their lives, Beth knew what such an accusation would do to her. Only the children thought of her as a witch. The people she blackmailed kept quiet, and the rest thought of her as a harmless old maker of potions. But once that dread word "witch" was thrown at her by someone as important as this viscount, she would be blamed for every bad harvest and every dead child and cow. And the villagers would take the law into their own hands.

"So hear this," Lord Granton went on. "If you so much as approach Miss Frederica Hadley again, I will make what is left of your life a misery, you wretched old crone."

"I swear to God," she cried, raising trembling hands, "that I only meant to give missie a fright to point out the folly of her ways."

He walked to the door while she shuffled after

him. "I do not believe your lies. I think you are malicious and evil."

Beth stood there after he had left. Her heart was thumping erratically, and her breath came out in ragged gasps. The heat of the small room suddenly seemed stifling. She could not seem to get a breath of air. She started to stagger, put out a hand to save herself, and then fell headlong to the floor, where she died of a seizure within minutes.

Lord Granton had been seen going into Beth's cottage, and speculation ran around the village as to the nature of his visit. Most assumed he had heard of her and wished to have his fortune told.

And then as Frederica sat that afternoon in the parlor of the rectory with her mother and sisters, their maid burst in, her eyes wide with excitement. "Old Beth Judge has been found dead!" she cried. "Lord Granton visited her and she's been found dead."

"Tish, girl," cried Mrs. Hadley. "Watch your tongue. You'll be saying he murdered her."

" 'Tis most odd that he should call and then her drop dead like that."

"I had better tell Dr. Hadley," said Mrs. Hadley. "He will need to arrange the laying out and burial."

Frederica sat very still, her head bent over a book. She saw not one word; all the time her mind cried out, "What has he done?"

She excused herself and hurried up to her room so that she could think more clearly. Relief and fear warred in her bosom: relief that the threat had been removed, fear that he had struck the old woman down. What did she really know of him? Why had she brushed aside his wicked reputation?

She should forget about him. She hugged herself and shivered despite the heat of the day. She had been playing a dangerous game, meeting him secretly. Why should she have had to meet him secretly? To all intents and purposes, everyone thought he was destined to be Annabelle's husband. Never having been jealous in her life, Frederica did not recognize her own jealousy of Annabelle, Annabelle who could converse with him openly, have him under her roof, walk with him and talk with him in the sunlight for all to see.

No, she would not meet him that evening or any other evening. She would go to the ball. In that wonderful gown and with her hair up, she might attract some man, some amiable man who might want to marry her. She tried to dream of such a man, but the viscount's wicked face kept rising before her eyes.

Over their early evening meal, Dr. Hadley suddenly said, "I have been at pains to go about the village putting down a most wicked piece of gossip that old Beth's death was anything to do with Lord Granton. The physician has examined her and she died of a seizure. She was nearly eighty, a great age, and beyond our Lord's appointed three score years and ten. People have strange and puzzling reactions. Mrs. Andrews, the baker's wife, burst into tears when she heard the news and cried, 'Thank God she is dead. My prayers have been answered.' "

Frederica wondered briefly if Mrs. Andrews had been threatened also with something by Beth, for surely the old woman had not suddenly taken to blackmail. But it seemed as if Lord Granton had had nothing at all to do with the death. Relief slowly seeped through her body. She had been picking at her food; now she suddenly began to eat with an appetite. She *would* meet him that evening.

Mrs. Hadley uneasily watched Frederica. Why, the girl looked radiant, beautiful. She could not remember Frederica ever looking so well. She thought of telling her she was not to go to the ball, thought of all that radiance dimmed, thought of strange Frederica's incalculable reaction, and felt a burst of anger against her husband. Why should *she* be left with the dismal chore of breaking the news to Frederica? Her husband should do it.

But Dr. Hadley had fallen grim and silent. She wondered why he looked so forbidding.

Dr. Hadley was remembering a small stack of letters he had found in a chest in old Beth's cottage when he had been going through her things to make sure there was nothing of value that might unaccountably go missing. They betrayed that the baker's wife had once had a romantic affair with Hal Turpin, a farm laborer, and that Agnes Dunn, the miller's daughter, had, while still a maiden, given birth to an illegitimate stillborn child. In some of the letters the women had pleaded that they could afford no more. He had burned the letters and gone to tell them so. He had not been at all surprised at Mrs. Andrews's reaction but had no intention of telling his wife about the real reason, or anyone else for that matter. He was also glad that the old woman had died a natural death, for had she not, he would have felt obliged to turn the letters over to the authorities.

He came out of his worried preoccupation to notice Frederica's radiant appearance. He kept shooting her puzzled little glances. Had it been any of his other daughters, he might have assumed her to be in love. But Frederica! He still thought of her as a child.

Frederica did not pause to think she might be falling in love with Lord Granton. She had always let her head rule her heart in every matter. Such as Lord Granton would never look on her as a marriageable prospect; she had been silly to become angry at the thought that she had to meet him in secret. It was a summer idyll, something to be remembered.

But she dressed with more than usual care and then on impulse braided her fine hair into a coronet on top of her head. She smiled at her reflection, pleased with the effect.

She ran down the back stairs and let herself out quietly into the evening calm of the garden. As she moved across the scrubby grass to the back gate, she felt she was walking onto a moonlit stage.

She must no longer get irritated with him, just enjoy the moment and think no further than the day after the ball when he would be gone from her life forever.

Chapter Six

Lord Granton let himself quietly into the darkness of the church. He drew back as he saw the elegant figure lit by a shaft of moonlight standing in the center of the aisle.

But, of course, it was Frederica. She turned and smiled at him. He caught his breath. She seemed a silver figure in the moonlight.

She walked to meet him. "Do you like my hair?" she asked, pirouetting slowly in front of him.

"Very fine." How odd that such a simple thing as putting her hair up had turned Frederica from a child into a young lady.

"Let us sit in one of the pews. Should anyone enter the church, we will not be observed." He opened the door of one of the high-walled pews. They sat side by side.

"I do not think that old woman will trouble you again," he began, "but should she do so, you must write to me in London or the country and I will come directly."

"You have not heard the news?" cried Frederica. "Mrs. Judge dropped dead of a seizure shortly after your visit. Did you threaten her?"

"I only told her that if she continued to trouble you I would report her as a witch."

"That must have frightened her to death," said Frederica. "There was an old woman in a village near here who was said to be a witch. The talk grew and grew, and soon every misfortune that happened to anyone in the village was blamed on her. She was driven out of her cottage. My father said she was harmless, only senile."

"I did not mean to frighten her that badly. On the other hand, I cannot mourn her death. If she tried to blackmail you, then it follows that she had been blackmailing other people."

"I believe that to be the case." Frederica looked down at her hands, suddenly shy. She wished they were back beside the pool, in the open air. Here, in the velvety darkness of the pew, she was intensely conscious of him, of the long, strong body so near her own.

"So this will be our last meeting before the ball," he said. "And then I shall be gone. Will you miss me?"

The Frederica of the pool would have given him a simple yes, but the Frederica in the dark proximity of the pew muttered, "Perhaps."

"Only perhaps?" he teased. "I shall miss you, Frederica."

"Take me with you." Frederica's voice was very low. He bent his head toward her.

"My child, it would be such a scandal."

"There is nothing for me here. You have had mistresses before."

"Experienced women of the world with little in the way of reputation to lose. It would not answer. You will soon marry and forget this summer interlude."

Not until I die, she thought. Why cannot he marry me? It would all be so simple. She realized clearly for the first time that when he went, he would take her heart with him.

They were silent. Lord Granton's conscience had never troubled him before so fiercely as it was doing at that moment. He felt as evil as he was reputed to be, sitting in this ancient church with this virgin, meeting her on the sly. He gave himself a mental shake. He had done nothing that was wrong . . . by the letter of the law. They had not been found out, except by one poacher who would not dare to open his mouth and by one old woman, now dead. Tomorrow was the ball and the day after he would go.

He could not see her new appearance in the darkness, and so he conjured up the girlish Frederica with her hair down her back.

"What shall we talk about?" he asked lightly. "What have you been reading?"

"I have been reading some interesting articles on India. One writer complains bitterly about the rise of the half-caste children in Bengal."

"And why is that?"

"Apart from the moral question, the writer argues that everywhere this intermediate caste has been allowed to rise it has been that land's ruin. Spanish America is an example of this. He fears that in India this tribe may soon become too powerful to control. He proposes that every father of half-caste children should be obliged to send them to Europe for their education and leave them there."

"And what about the ruin of Europe? Oh, I see. He feels this new breed might throw the British masters out of India?"

"I assume that is what he is saying. He says many are sent to England for their education but then are brought back to work in the mercantile houses."

"I think perhaps religion might bring about the end of our rule in India. There is great resentment among the Hindus over the efforts of the missionaries. They should have followed the advice of the Duke of Wellington when he was in India and he ordered his troops not to interfere with either the religions or customs of that country."

She fell silent again and he looked down on her shadowy figure, half in exasperation, half with affection. Poor Frederica. What gentleman was ever going to let her talk freely about half-caste children without being deeply shocked? Ladies were not even supposed to know about such matters. And how boring that did make them.

"How goes Miss Annabelle?" asked Frederica.

"Restored to health and spirits. It is my belief that were it not for this ball, she would have languished prettily in bed, eating grapes and enjoying her invalid status for several weeks."

"Perhaps Papa might be persuaded to take the little money that is set aside for my dowry and send me to India," said Frederica.

"Think of the heat! Think of the dreadful journey!"

"But it would be an adventure," said Frederica patiently. "There was an advertisement in the newspapers. An elderly lady in Calcutta advertised for a young companion, provided said companion was prepared to pay her own passage."

"And what if the old lady should die before you got there? Calcutta is only bearable if one is leading a social life, and as companion to an old lady, you might find your days even more boring than they are here."

"One should take risks, I think," said Frederica sententiously. "It could be another scene entirely. She could be a very amiable, very rich old lady who would be so grateful that she would leave me her fortune, and then I might be able to marry an army officer and lead a dashing life."

"From what I have heard, life in Calcutta is hardly dashing. One rises early to enjoy the cool air, such as there is. Then one has tiffin, a hot meal which is taken at noon. Then bed for three or four hours. Then when it grows dark, everyone dresses, despite the stifling heat, in English style and goes out to eat long stultifying dinners during which all the men become abominably drunk."

"You do not offer hope for any romance in this life. I shall not tell you more of my ideas," said Frederica crossly.

"You will have romance enough tomorrow night when you dance at the ball. Have you been practicing your steps?"

"Yes, as often as I can."

"Good girl," he said absently. And then after a few moments of heavy silence, he said reluctantly, "I should go. I would be very sad if we were to be discovered before the ball."

Frederica felt him preparing to make a move. She suddenly said breathlessly, "May I ask you a favor?"

"If it is in my power, I will grant it."

"Will you kiss me?"

"Frederica! Why?"

"Because I have never been kissed by a gentleman before and probably will not be ever in my whole life."

"Do you mean you wish me to kiss you on the lips?"

Frederica gave a shaky laugh. "Where else?"

His long fingers felt for her face in the darkness and then cradled it in his hands. Slowly his lips descended on hers in a gentle kiss. She was suddenly shaken with passion, with a burning heat. The passion seemed to be surging up through her body to her lips.

He felt her lips against his own, cool and virginal and sweet. He was about to draw away when suddenly those lips beneath his own started to burn and cling. His senses went whirling around and he kissed her more deeply, his mouth fused against hers.

And then the church clock far above their heads chimed the quarter hour and he drew back, his breathing ragged.

They rose together. He held open the door of the pew for her. Side by side they walked down the aisle, pausing in the darkness of the church porch.

"Until tomorrow," he whispered.

"Until tomorrow," she echoed faintly.

He walked away through the slanting tombstones. She stood where she was, watching him go, wondering whether it might be possible to die from an excess of sweetness mixed with pain and loss.

Lord Granton walked slowly back to the Hall, bewildered and confused. Frederica! Little Frederica, of all people to inspire such passion in him!

He should not have kissed her like that, but the sweetness of her lips kept returning to him. And then he struck his forehead and said aloud, "Why, what a fool I am! All I have to do is marry the girl."

The more he thought about marrying Frederica, the more exciting the whole idea seemed. He felt like a youth again. He would ask Dr. Hadley at the ball to be allowed to pay his addresses, and then he would make the announcement. His conscience told him that it was a cruel thing to do to Annabelle, but it would no doubt drive Annabelle into the arms of the major. Frederica, after all the slights and snubs and humiliations she had received, would have her moment of triumph.

Meanwhile Frederica let herself into the rectory by the front door. There was no need to sneak round the back. She could say, truthfully, that she had visited the church.

"Is that you, Frederica?" called her mother's voice from the parlor. "Come in here."

Frederica entered the parlor, blinking in the light. Her sisters stared at the "new" Frederica, with her elegant coronet of braided hair.

"Come and sit down by me," said Mrs. Hadley in a strained voice. Her eyes were red with weeping. The enormity of breaking the news of the banishment from the ball to Frederica at this last minute had struck her, and again she had pleaded with her husband to help her to tell the girl, but Dr. Hadley had said it was her job to do so and had locked himself in his study.

Frederica sat down and smiled all around, still dazed from that kiss.

"Frederica, I must tell you, you are not to go to the ball. Lady Crown has forbidden it."

"I beg your pardon, Mama?" Frederica smiled vaguely round the room, not having heard a word.

"I said, you are not to go to the ball," repeated Mrs. Hadley in a shrill voice. "And you brought it on yourself with that stupid lie about typhoid."

"Mama!" exclaimed Mary. "What is this? Why weren't we told?"

"Because Frederica might have gone further, might have said something even more dreadful, and then we would all have been stopped from going!"

In a thin little voice, Frederica said, "Are you saying that I am not invited, that you knew of this, and yet you have waited until this moment to tell me?"

Amy and Harriet sat wide-eyed. They could think of no worse punishment in the world than being forbidden to go to the ball at Townley Hall.

"You are so incalculable," wailed Mrs. Hadley. "Besides, you have never really been interested in such things."

Frederica sat there, bewildered. All the gladness and wonder she had felt over that kiss had fled to be replaced by a deep depression. She was only silly little Frederica Hadley from the rectory, not marriageable, who did not know how to behave to her betters and was being punished accordingly.

Mary stood up. "I shall not go," she announced, striking her breast. "I shall stay here tomorrow night with my little sister."

"Oh, that is stoopid!" cried Amy. "Frederica brought this on herself and nearly stopped us going as well."

Frederica stood up. "Good night," she said abruptly. She turned and walked from the room. Mary, Mary of all people, to make such a generous offer. That was really what had finally overset her. She ran to her room and threw herself on the bed and cried until she could cry no more.

Lord Granton awoke the next day with an unusual feeling of happiness and anticipation flooding through him. He wondered if he should tell his friend, the major, that he was to marry Frederica. But the softhearted major might tell the Crowns, and he did want Frederica to have her moment of triumph. Besides, the Crowns had no reason to expect him to propose marriage. He had made no advances to Annabelle, nor had he asked Sir Giles for his permission to pay his addresses to her.

He had anticipated a day free of social duties before the ball, but at breakfast Sir Giles said cheerfully, "Poor Annabelle, although quite recovered from her ordeal, would benefit from some fresh air, and the day is fine. There is nothing she can do here to help with the preparations. My wife will do it all." Which meant that Lady Crown would supervise an army of servants and caterers. "Why do you not take her for a drive?"

"Good idea," said the major, to Lord Granton's relief. "I will come, too."

Lady Crown frowned. "That will not be necessary. I would like you to stay and advise me on some matters, Major."

Annabelle dimpled at Lord Granton. "I will not be very long."

That meant an hour while Annabelle's maid helped her into a new carriage gown and rearranged her hair.

"Where would you like to go?" asked Lord Granton somewhat ungraciously when they were seated in one of the Hall's curricles.

Annabelle pouted. She felt her company ought to be enough. "Just around and about," she said.

He set out at a smart pace, wishing it were Frederica beside him. Annabelle prattled on about the fine weather and how she would like to sketch that vista of trees and fields over there.

"I know a very pretty pool quite near here," he said.

"The one at Cummins Woods? But you cannot drive to it. One has to walk."

"I am sure a short walk will not harm either of us." He had never thought of himself as a sentimental man, but he suddenly wanted a last look at the pool beside which he had talked to Frederica and taught her to dance.

Frederica awoke to a dismal day. Once more life stretched out in front of her, flat and dark. But as she washed and dressed, she decided she would go to that pool to see if she could recapture some happy memories that were not tinged with shame. *She* had asked him to kiss *her!*

And he had not uttered one word of love. He would regard her with amusement as just another conquest. Only look at his reputation. He had been amusing himself with her, passing a boring visit to the country. Would he miss her at the ball? He obviously had not known she was not to go. But perhaps he would be relieved she was not there.

She joined her family for breakfast. "Why, Mama," she said sadly, "did you not warn me I was not to go? I have that beautiful ball gown, and now I will never have a chance to wear it."

"As to that," said Dr. Hadley, "you will be able to wear it to winter assemblies in Evesham."

"And Dr. Hadley has suggested we engage the services of a dancing master for you," said Mrs. Hadley.

Frederica picked at her food. Her unruly tongue! "And it was because I said there was typhoid in the village," she said.

Mrs. Hadley nodded. "Then we were all re-invited, but not you. My dear child, what if I had told you then? You might have met the Crowns and said something else and then your poor sisters would be banned as well."

"I shall not go," said Mary stoutly. "I think it is most unfair. We shall have a cozy evening here, and I will read you my poems, Frederica."

Frederica was about to remark that she had no wish to listen to poems plagiarized from the *Ladies' Magazine* but then realized the kindness of her elder sister's gesture and said instead, "You are very good, Mary. But it would give me much more pleasure to think of you at that ball. Come now. You can write a splendid poem about it all and read it to me later."

Mary's face registered a conflict of desires. She really felt that Frederica should not be left behind alone, and yet she did long to go.

"I will wait up for you all," urged Frederica, "and you can tell me about it."

"In that case . . . ," said Mary.

"Of course you should go," snapped Harriet. "I, for one, am not sorry for Frederica at all. She is only getting what she deserves."

There was a silence. Frederica drank some chocolate and nibbled at some toast. She felt in some way she was being punished for having been so vain, so stupid. For she had begun to hope that Lord Granton might have come to love her. She had to admit that now. And in the clear light of day, with the sun streaming in through the old mullioned windows of the rectory, her behavior began to seem to her disgraceful. Using her father's church for an assignation and then begging one of London's most famous rakes to kiss her!

And yet, still she decided to go back to that pool.

Lord Granton and Annabelle stood in silence, side by side, looking at the pool, each immersed in private thoughts.

I hope we spend most of the year in London when we are married, Annabelle was thinking. The country is so tiresome. All those lovely shops in London, and all the balls and routs and theaters. She supposed he had brought her here to kiss her. Annabelle had never been kissed and wondered what it would be like. Only think of his reputation. What if he went too far?

A smile curved Lord Granton's lips as he thought of Frederica. When they were married, they would come to this spot again and remember it was where he taught her to dance, and they would laugh over how stupid he had been to waste so much time meeting her in secret when all he had to do was to ask her father for permission to pay his addresses.

"Are you enjoying your visit to the country?" he realized Annabelle was asking.

"Oh, immensely," he said, smiling down at her. "In fact, I cannot remember when I have enjoyed myself more."

"My lord, you flatter me."

He looked at her modestly lowered eyelashes, and said, rather curtly, "I did not mean to flatter you. The countryside around here is very beautiful."

She gave him a startled look but then decided she could not have heard him correctly. She moved close to him and put a confiding hand on his arm. "You must admit Town is a much more fascinating place."

"On the contrary, I am tired of London and I think I would prefer to stay in the country."

"But one would go to Town for the Season!"

"I am sure you will enjoy another Season."

So that meant he at least would take her to

London every Season, thought Annabelle.

"I should like that above all things," she said.

Her grip on his arm grew tighter, and she gazed up into his face.

And that is how Frederica saw them as she came quietly through the woods. They looked an intimate couple. A hot wave of shame engulfed her, and she turned and moved quietly away.

She walked rapidly home and crept up the back stairs to her room, her only sanctuary now, as all her favorite places had become tainted with his presence and with what she saw as the betrayal of her feelings. He had used her as a momentary diversion while his well-ordered life of courtship and proposal to Annabelle went ahead. That he had taken Annabelle to *their* pool showed that all their meetings had meant nothing to him. She was now beyond tears and very glad that she was not to go to the ball. How would she have reacted when she heard the announcement of his engagement to Annabelle? Better to endure her shame and misery alone and in private.

Lady Crown, seeing that all the preparations for the ball were well under way, decided to broach the delicate question of Lord Granton to her daughter. If Lord Granton meant to announce his engagement to Annabelle at the ball, there had certainly been no sign of it. Surely the viscount would have told Sir Giles by now of his intentions.

When she saw Annabelle returning from her

drive with Lord Granton, she waited until her daughter was in her private sitting room and went to confront her.

"You must not be too disappointed, my dear," began Lady Crown as Annabelle removed her bonnet and passed it to her maid. "You may leave us," snapped Lady Crown to the maid. "I have private matters to discuss with my daughter."

When the maid had curtsied her way out, Lady Crown said, "Sit down, my dear. I fear we must face facts. Granton is not going to propose to you. He said something last night about taking his leave immediately after the ball."

Annabelle laughed. "Much you know of it, Mama. I asked him if we would spend much time in London, and he replied that he favored country life but that he would take me to the Season."

"He said that! Oh, my little love, I am so proud of you. To think my little daughter has succeeded where so many have failed! But is it not sad that he has said nothing to your father?"

"He probably wants it to be a surprise," said Annabelle, "and it might come as a surprise to everyone — except me."

The doting mother promptly forgot about her daughter's singular failure to attract a suitor at the previous Season. Her pride and vanity were every bit as great as that of her daughter, and her momentary flash of common sense had gone. They were, after all, the Crowns of Barton Sub

Edge, a worthy family. Lord Granton was a lucky man.

"Where did you go on your drive, my dear?"

"That pool in Cummins Woods. Such a dreary spot. But gentlemen are so odd in their tastes." Annabelle gave a triumphant little laugh. "But I shall soon reform him. I declare I feel in such charity with the world that I have a mind to let that tiresome little girl, Frederica, come to the ball after all."

"She deserves to be punished."

"Oh, what does it matter? Let her come."

Annabelle was still piqued that Frederica had commanded so much of Lord Granton's attention during that visit to the rectory. Frederica should be at the ball to witness the betrothal of herself to Lord Granton. "Besides," she went on, "it might be remarked upon were she the one Hadley daughter not to be invited."

"As you wish, my love. I shall send a footman to the rectory with an invitation. But mark my words, it is more than Frederica Hadley deserves."

"You *what?*" The major stood stock still and gazed openmouthed at his friend. They had been walking across the lawns in front of the Hall when Lord Granton dropped his bombshell, his desire to confide in someone overriding his earlier caution. "You mean to marry that odd child from the rectory?"

"Yes, I do. Wish me well."

"No, I will not wish you well," declared the major, his temper rising. "I have a bad feeling you are expected to announce your engagement to Annabelle."

"They have no reason to believe that. Have I declared my intentions?"

"No, but . . ." The major looked sharply at his friend. "But it is a wonder the news of your forthcoming engagement is not all over the village. I cannot imagine such as Mrs. Hadley keeping quiet about that!"

"It is because they do not yet know."

"You are immoral!" raged the major. "Why should you cause your hosts such distress and shock the Hadleys? They will surely want to know why you should wish to marry their youngest daughter. Have you been meeting her on the sly?"

"I have been meeting her, yes."

"Then why did you not simply ask her father's permission? She will surely have told her parents herself."

Lord Granton had the grace to color up.

"You mean you haven't told her? Such arrogance! You expect her to fall into your arms and say yes?"

"She is not indifferent to me. I love her. She has been humiliated and passed over. I want to give her her moment of triumph."

"You are like Lord Byron — mad, bad, and dangerous to know. I am dreading this evening.

You are behaving cruelly and irresponsibly toward that angel."

"Frederica?"

"No!" howled the major, quite beside himself with fury. "Annabelle."

"You are becoming exercised over nothing. Have I even held her hand, murmured sweet nothings to her, sought out her company? No, I have not."

"Then let me tell you this. I feel honor bound to tell Miss Annabelle quite definitely that you are not going to propose to her!"

"I do not want you to mention Frederica's name! They would stop her from attending."

"No, but I will put her wise to your lack of honorable intentions."

The major strode off and Lord Granton ruefully watched him go. He admitted to himself that he was behaving irresponsibly. But it was only a few hours now until the ball, and all would be resolved.

Ten minutes later the major found Annabelle in the ballroom, or the chain of salons which was to be the ballroom, supervising the French chalking of the floor. Ballroom floors in the best houses were not simply chalked. Colored chalks were used to make an elaborate pattern of flowers and fruit on the floor despite the fact that the whole artistic effect would be ruined by the arrival of the first guests.

"Miss Annabelle!" cried the major, his round

face flushed with distress. "I beg a moment of your time."

"But of course, Major," said Annabelle, smiling on him sweetly, for she knew the major adored her and was therefore behaving just as a gentleman ought.

He drew her out of earshot of the busy servants and the "artist" from the village who was laboriously drawing out patterns on the floor.

"I do not like to be the bringer of bad news," said the major. "I am ashamed to tell you that my friend, Lord Granton, is not going to propose to you."

Annabelle surveyed him with a certain irritation. "Major, you really must pull yourself together. There is nothing to become excited about. You have already tried to tell me this."

"There is! There is! I feel he has been playing fast and loose with the most beautiful lady I have ever met. Oh, Miss Annabelle, I love you from the bottom of my poor heart. Pray, be mine! You refused me before, but now I tell you, Lord Granton most definitely does not mean to propose to you."

And to Annabelle's consternation, the major sank down onto one knee in front of the curious stares of the servants.

"Control yourself, sir." Annabelle backed away as the major tried to grasp her hand. "I am flattered by your proposal but must decline it. Do behave, dear sir, and go and drink a seltzer water."

"But, Miss Annabelle . . . !" The major, red-faced, stumbled clumsily to his feet.

"I said, enough!" cried Annabelle, who was now thoroughly enjoying herself. She had never felt more beautiful, more irresistible, more powerful. She plucked a rose from a vase and held it out to the poor major, who took it and clutched it to his breast. "Now, begone!" Annabelle struck an Attitude she had seen in London that was meant to represent a princess repulsing the attentions of an unwanted suitor, one hand outstretched, the other to her brow. Still clutching the rose, the major walked away. And then he suddenly found himself becoming angry.

Annabelle deserved a good set-down, he thought suddenly, and Lord Granton would see that she got it!

Mrs. Hadley's hands trembled as she opened the sealed letter that had arrived from the Hall. Now what? Were they all to be banned, and at the very last minute?

She read the contents and then let out a little shriek. Then she ran into her husband's study. "Dr. Hadley!" she cried. "Such a surprise! A letter, a charming letter from Lady Crown. She feels Frederica has been punished enough and has graciously said she may attend. What do you think of that?"

Dr. Hadley sat very still, looking wearily at his wife. "I am not in a position to feel other than gratified. Frederica will have to be forced to go to that wretched ball."

"What can you mean, sir?"

"I mean that Frederica will consider the lateness and tone of the invitation an insult." He held up his hand. "And she will be right. But in my position, I dare not offend the Crowns. You must let me talk to Frederica myself. I will do it now."

He rose slowly to his feet. "It is difficult, my dear, in our financial situation, to care for four daughters. But I fear we have treated Frederica more like a poor relation than a daughter."

"But she is so young, little more than a child."

"I have lately observed she has become a young lady. She has a fine ball gown. Make sure her hair is put up as befits her age and that she has any embellishments for her ensemble she requires."

Frederica was sitting in her favorite chair by the window of her room when her father entered.

"Papa." She rose dutifully. "Nothing is amiss, I trust?"

"I fear you are going to think it so. My child, Lady Crown has graciously decided that you may attend the ball this evening after all."

Color flared up in Frederica's face. "Never!" she said passionately.

"Sit down, Frederica, and listen to me and listen carefully. I know you often feel that we toady quite dreadfully to the Crowns. In my case, it is because of fears that they might remove my living, and then what would become of us? Lady

Crown is so proud and yet has a flightiness of mind. Were you not to attend, that might be regarded as an insult. I cannot risk that. In our position in life, which we must always remember was given to us by the good Lord, we must respect the whims and foibles of our betters. So you must go, Frederica."

She turned away from him and looked out the window. The weather was still fine, the sun still shone, intensifying the darkness she felt within her.

If she went, she would hear him announce his engagement to Annabelle. But perhaps that would be a good thing, would increase her contempt for him. It would be an opportunity to show him how little she cared.

She turned back and said in a flat voice, "Very well, Papa. But I shall wear my hair up."

"Of course, and your mother and sisters will gladly lend you anything you require. It is only a ball, my dear. You look quite white."

"I shall do very well," said Frederica.

When her father had left, she sat down again. If only she could forget that kiss, which had meant so much to her and so little to him. She sat there for a long time, and finally with a little shrug she got to her feet. She would work on her appearance as she had never worked on it before. Lord Granton would not know her heart was breaking.

Dr. Hadley left the church just before he was

due back at the rectory for the early evening meal. His conscience was troubling him. He had not liked the way in which Frederica had been invited at the very last minute, but he did not see what he could possibly do about it. He gave a little sigh as he emerged from the darkness of the church porch and nearly collided with the tall figure of Lord Granton.

"My lord," he said with a gasp of surprise, "you startled me."

"I am sorry, Rector; I have come to confess my sins."

The rector looked anxiously at his turnip-sized watch, which he drew out from his pocket. He was gratified at the request but felt uneasily that the sins of Lord Granton might take quite a long time to listen to. "Perhaps," he ventured, "we could set a time for tomorrow? I am on my way to dinner, and then there are all the preparations to go to the ball, and . . ."

"It will not take long," said Lord Granton. "If we might step inside the church for a moment?"

"Very well." Dr. Hadley led the way back into the church. He turned in the center aisle to face Lord Granton. "Now, if I may be of assistance . . . ?"

"I wish to ask your leave to allow me to pay my addresses to your daughter."

The rector looked up at him in amazement. "Which daughter?"

"Frederica."

"*Frederica!* But you have only met her for a few moments."

"This is my confession. I have been meeting Frederica secretly."

Dr. Hadley's face hardened. "You shock me. This is outrageous. Her reputation will be ruined."

"Her reputation will not be ruined," said Lord Granton testily, "because I am going to marry the girl, if she will have me."

"But why did you meet her in secret? It was not necessary. She is a respectable girl. All you had to do was to ask my permission to pay court to her and you could have met her openly."

"My conscience is sore on that point." Lord Granton stared up at the church roof as if for inspiration. "She seemed to me to be little more than an intelligent child. She amused me. I was sorry for her because she was so neglected by you and your wife. Then I fell in love with her. You must forgive me for my strange behavior."

Dr. Hadley stared at him with mounting anger. "You are outrageous, my lord. You are a guest of the Crowns; you are fully expected to announce your engagement to Miss Annabelle Crown this very evening. The Crowns will feel slighted and furious should you announce your engagement to Frederica instead, and I will lose my living. Oh, I have seen by the look on your face that you think I creep and crawl to them dreadfully, but what else can I do?"

A mocking smile appeared on Lord Granton's

lips. "Dr. Hadley, you may lose a living but you will be gaining as a son-in-law one of the richest men in England."

"Oh, dear, so I shall," said Dr. Hadley. "Oh, so I shall."

"So you see, whether the Crowns disapprove or not, there is nothing they can do now to harm you. So I must ask you again, reminding you at the same time that you still have three daughters to bring out after Frederica, and with my patronage you will now be able to do so in style, may I marry your daughter?"

"Does Frederica accept you?"

"I have not yet asked her, but I will ask her at the ball. To be frank, I was furious at her treatment and did not wish to tell you anything until she had accepted me. I wanted her to be the star of the ball. I wanted to make it up to her for all the times she has been passed over, neglected, and humiliated. Come, Dr. Hadley, I think we both have much to be ashamed of in our treatment of Frederica."

Dr. Hadley held out his hand, and Lord Granton solemnly shook it. "I welcome you as a son-in-law," said the rector.

"I must crave your indulgence, sir. Do not tell your wife or daughters of this. I wish it to be a surprise."

Dr. Hadley gazed at him in a dazed way. The import of these glorious words, "one of the richest men in England," was slowly sinking in. God is rewarding me at last, thought Dr. Hadley.

"Yes, of course," he said. "It shall be our secret until tonight."

"Then I bid you good day, sir."

Lord Granton turned and strolled out of the church.

Dr. Hadley slowly followed. Security at last! It no longer mattered what the Crowns thought. Frederica, of all people, would be a viscountess. She would take precedence over Lady Crown.

When he entered the house, his face was so suffused with happiness that his wife observed sharply, "You look almost exalted."

"Something wonderful happened to me in the church. A revelation!" cried Dr. Hadley. He beamed at Frederica, who was sitting with her hair in clay rollers. Frederica looked bleakly back. She wished she could share what she understood to be her father's strong spiritual belief, for she had tried to pray for help but could only come to the dismal conclusion that an unforgiving God had sent down on her head the humiliation she so richly deserved for asking a rake to kiss her, and in the church, too!

Chapter Seven

Lord Granton smiled dreamily at his reflection in the mirror as he took a freshly starched and laundered cravat from his valet and proceeded to tie it carefully in the style known as The Oriental. He had finally done the correct thing. He had obtained Dr. Hadley's permission to marry Frederica.

The door of his dressing room crashed open and Major Harry Delisle walked in. "Leave us," he snapped at the valet.

Lord Granton swung round, his face darkening. "I hope you have a good explanation, Harry, for bursting in while I am dressing and dismissing my valet."

"You are a monster and no friend of mine," howled Harry. "That angel still believes you are going to marry her. But your perverted taste prefers the charms of a gauche schoolgirl young enough to be your daughter!"

"That's enough. Do not dare insult my future bride."

"I proposed to Annabelle and was rejected."

"Harry, I have obtained the good rector's permission to pay my addresses to his daughter, and that is that. We have stayed at country houses before. I have risen hopes before by my very presence. I always do. It is my title and my fortune, not my face or figure, that is always the attraction. Yes, I admit I have been behaving badly, but I am about to rectify the matter. Before you punch me, which you are obviously dying to do, think on this. Apart from a short drive this morning, I have always seen Annabelle in your presence. Have I ever done or said anything to raise her hopes?"

The major glared at him.

"No, think about it, Harry. I sometimes pay pretty young misses compliments; I sometimes flirt. It is the fashion. In the case of Annabelle Crown, I have done neither of those things. And how did she reject your suit? Triumphantly, I should think. Did she strike an Attitude?"

The major now scowled at the carpet, remembering that outstretched hand and the other to her brow in such a theatrical way.

"I thought so," said the viscount, reading his silence for assent. "So instead of concentrating on my bad behavior, what of the behavior of a young miss whose vanity leaves her impervious to every coldness? A good set-down might do her the world of good."

That was what the major had been thinking earlier, but his pride had reasserted itself and he had become convinced that Annabelle would have accepted him had it not been for his friend's disgraceful ways.

"I am sorry," said Lord Granton ruefully. "I feel you are so anxious to be wed, Harry, that you are ready to fall in love with anyone. And if you married Annabelle, you would not see much of her, for she would not be the sort of army wife to go with you." He finished tying his cravat. "Now, you look very fine. Let us go downstairs. You will not believe me at the moment, but such as Annabelle Crown is not worth losing a good friend."

They walked in silence out of the room and along the passage that led to the main staircase.

As they passed Annabelle's rooms, they heard her trill of laughter. "Can you believe it, Mama?" came her voice with dreadful clarity, for the door was slightly ajar. "There was that funny, fat little major down on one knee with all the servants staring. I was hard put not to laugh."

And Lady Crown replied, "You will break hearts tonight. You are so very beautiful."

"I think you have heard enough," said Lord Granton quietly. He put his hand under the major's arm and urged him forward.

"Where is Frederica?" demanded Mrs. Hadley shrilly as she, her husband, and her three other daughters waited impatiently in the rectory drawing room. "If we are late, we will offend the Crowns."

"A pox on the Crowns," said the rector happily. "Let them wait."

"Dr. Hadley! Such language, and in front of your daughters, too!"

The door opened and Frederica came in. Her family stared at her in amazement. She had cleverly copied one of the new Roman hairstyles from a fashion magazine and threaded her mother's seed pearls through it. The new ball gown shimmered with little pearls in the candlelight of the drawing room. Her face was delicately flushed, and her eyes were very wide and dark.

Dr. Hadley walked forward and held out his arm. "You look like a princess." Frederica smiled vaguely and put her hand on his arm. "Shall we go?" she said quietly.

They climbed into the old rectory carriage, driven for the evening by a man from the village. The sun was setting, sending great slanting shafts of sunlight over the tussocky grass of the churchyard.

"I think you look a trifle too modish and grand, Frederica," said Mary, all her good intentions and feelings toward this youngest sister eradicated in a burst of jealousy. "The Crowns will think you are getting above your station." Dr. Hadley gave a happy laugh, and Frederica looked at him anxiously, wondering if her father was drunk.

All she wanted to do was to get through this terrible evening ahead with as much dignity as possible.

Townley Hall was a blaze of lights from top to bottom as their old carriage, pulled by their old horse, moved slowly up the drive. Amy and Harriet began to shift and giggle nervously. "Do you think Lord Granton will dance with one of us?" asked Harriet.

"What does it matter if he does?" demanded Mary waspishly. "He will announce his engagement, and Annabelle will preen and smile and toss her head. She will be a viscountess, and her pride will be beyond bearing."

"I *am* so looking forward to this evening," said Dr. Hadley. "There will be no one there to match Frederica."

"Papa, are you feeling quite the thing?" asked Frederica anxiously.

"Never better, my child."

"You look very well, Frederica," remarked Mrs. Hadley sharply. "You look like a lady for the first time. I beg of you, please behave like one."

The carriage stopped at the entrance to the hall and they all alighted.

They walked up the main staircase, where the ladies made their curtsies to Sir Giles and Lady Crown, who were standing at the top to greet the guests.

Lady Crown's eyes narrowed when she saw Frederica. "Dear me," she said acidly, "how did you come by that gown? It is much too fine for a little girl of your social position."

"We shall all pretend we did not hear that very rude remark," said the rector. He urged his distressed wife forward. "Come, my dear."

"Dr. Hadley, are you run mad?" wailed Mrs. Hadley. "She was furious."

"And so am I," said Dr. Hadley. "Irritating old hag."

"Oh, you *are* drunk," moaned Mrs. Hadley. "Pray guard your tongue and I will later see if I can repair the damage." She pinned a social smile on her lips. She must apologize to Lady Crown at the earliest opportunity. And to think she had always wondered where Frederica got her sharp tongue and odd behavior from.

Frederica felt naked. Everyone seemed to be staring at her. And then Lord Granton came straight up to her and bowed low. "May I have the honor of this dance?"

"It is the waltz," said Mrs. Hadley, flustered. "I do not think our little Frederica can . . . I mean, perhaps Mary here . . ."

But Frederica moved off with Lord Granton, and soon she was pirouetting in his arms.

"How could you?" demanded Frederica.

"How could I what?"

"You took her to *my* pool, and you held her hand, and now the place is *contaminated.*"

"Annabelle had her hand on my arm. I was not holding her hand. You look so beautiful, but you are being frightfully silly."

And Frederica Hadley detached herself from him, drew back her hand, and slapped him full across the face.

Behind her, on the edge of the dance floor, Mrs. Hadley swooned. Frederica turned and ran.

Lord Granton stood for a moment looking after her fleeing figure and then he set out in pursuit.

Frederica ran straight out of the front door, past the staring footmen, and down the drive. She was halfway down it when he caught up with her and swung her around.

"What was all that about, you hellcat? How dare you strike me."

"How dare you philander? How dare you lead me on? How dare you kiss me?"

"I kissed you because you asked me to!"

"You should have refused," said Frederica, tears starting in her eyes.

The anger left his face and he said softly, "What a clumsy fool I have been. What an idiot. Did you never guess that I had fallen in love with you, Frederica?"

Her eyes were great pools in the dusk. "How can you say you love me?" she asked brokenly. "If you loved me, you would have courted me properly, but you did not consider me worth it. You would have spoken to my father. . . ."

He gave her a little shake. "I have, I did. He says I can marry you."

"Marry *you?*"

"Oh, Frederica, you must marry me. How was I to know I would finally fall in love? I should have asked you; I should have asked your father this age. Forgive me, sweeting, for I cannot take no for an answer."

She wound her arms around his neck and said softly in a wondering voice, "Can this be true?

You want me as your wife?"

"Oh, yes, my little love. But if you strike me again, I will strangle you and create even more of a scandal."

She suddenly smiled. "Then kiss me instead, Rupert."

He swept her into his arms and bent his dark head. His lips found hers. He pressed her to his body, and Frederica returned his passion until they were both breathing raggedly.

"Now, then," he said at last, "we had better return so that I may make a respectable woman of you." He tucked her hand into his arm.

Frederica began to laugh. "Poor Papa. That was why he was so rude to Lady Crown. After seeing me slap your face, he must be worried to death."

Dr. Hadley, his shoulders stooped, stood humbly before Lady Crown. "I cannot apologize more for my daughter's behavior," he said.

"It is your own behavior which was every bit as reprehensible," said Lady Crown awfully. "I said to Sir Giles that we cannot possibly entertain such a clergyman in our parish and he agreed."

Dr. Hadley reflected dismally that after Frederica's behavior there was no way Lord Granton would marry her, and no point in explaining to the dreadful Crowns that he had meant to do so. Mrs. Hadley, recovered from her swoon, was sobbing quietly beside him. "What will become of us?" she said in a choked voice.

"I neither know nor care," said Lady Crown with every appearance of enjoyment. "We are furious that such a distinguished guest should be insulted in this way. Annabelle is sorely distressed. I would suggest that you leave our home and take your daughters with you, Dr. Hadley."

Mrs. Hadley was only too glad to comply. But Harriet and Amy were dancing, and she would need to wait until the quadrille had finished before telling them they must leave.

Just as the dance finished, Frederica walked into the ballroom on the arm of Lord Granton. Lady Crown sailed forward majestically. Frederica Hadley deserved the public humiliation she was about to get.

"My dear Lord Granton," she fluted, "let me take this rude and stupid girl to her parents so that she may go home and disgrace herself no longer." The music had stopped. Everyone was listening. Amy, Harriet, and Mary, their faces scarlet with mortification, stood beside their tearful mother and a strained and worried Dr. Hadley.

"Miss Frederica Hadley was much provoked by me," said Lord Granton loudly, "but our quarrel is over, and she has done me the great honor, the *very* great honor, of agreeing to become my wife."

Annabelle stepped forward, the ostrich feathers on her head trembling, every flounce on her pink muslin gown seeming to bristle with outrage.

"This is some mad joke," she declared shrilly.

"You are to marry me! Me! You promised."

"I promised nothing, nor did I pay you any particular attention," said Lord Granton, putting an arm about Frederica's shoulders.

Annabelle stamped her foot. "You said we should go to London for every Season when we were married. You said so. Just today."

"I said nothing of the kind, Miss Crown. If I remember rightly, you said that *one* went to London for the Season, and I agreed as I assumed your parents would be taking you back for another Season."

"But Frederica of all people!" shouted Annabelle. "You cannot want to marry Frederica. Why?"

"Because I love her." Lord Granton smiled all around. "Wish me well. I am the luckiest man alive."

The Hadleys surged forward, Mrs. Hadley crying, "Oh, my *bestest* of daughters. But why did you not call? How could you have come to know Frederica?"

"Dr. Hadley will explain," said Lord Granton. "I asked him permission to press my suit and he agreed."

Sir Giles then joined them. "Lord Granton, you led my poor daughter on. I wish you to leave my house immediately."

Dr. Hadley beamed. "We have room enough at the rectory, my lord."

"Then take my future bride home, and Major Delisle and I will join you shortly."

They were about to leave the ballroom when Annabelle approached them again. She looked only at the major. "A word with you, Major Delisle," she said.

"I really don't think . . ." The major's voice trailed away as he watched the retreating backs of the Hadleys, escorted by Lord Granton.

"I have decided to accept your offer of marriage," said Annabelle. She smiled on him. "Ah, you look startled. But you shall have your reward."

"You turned me down," said the major. "I made a mistake. Let's forget about the whole thing." And with that, he hurried after Lord Granton.

The Hadley family seemed in a state of shock as they were driven homeward. Lord Granton and the major were to follow with their luggage. Mrs. Hadley kept exclaiming over and over again that Frederica, of all people, should become a viscountess. Then she began to worry about rooms to be prepared for these unexpected guests. A room would also have to be found for Gustave, Lord Granton's man.

"It's all very well for Frederica," grumbled Amy. "But we are to be left here after you are wed, Frederica, to live with the Crowns' wrath — that is, if they let Papa keep the living after this."

"Lord Granton told me that as he is one of the richest men in England, I need no longer fear the Crowns," said Dr. Hadley happily. "And he will see to it that the rest of my daughters make their come-out at the Season."

"God is indeed good," announced Mary, but Harriet and Amy let out squeals of delight and began to beg Frederica to tell them how on earth Lord Granton had come to know her so well as to want to marry her.

But Mrs. Hadley cut across their chatter by demanding of her husband, "Lord Granton had obviously asked your permission, Dr. Hadley. Why did you not warn me? Why did you say nothing?"

"He wanted it kept a secret," said Dr. Hadley. "He wanted our little Frederica to have her moment of triumph after what he saw as our shabby treatment of her."

"But we did not treat her shabbily," wailed Mrs. Hadley. "Frederica, such was not the case. Oh, dear, with four daughters, what did he expect?"

But Frederica was in too happy a daze to go in for recriminations. Mrs. Hadley surveyed her, wondering if she had ever really known this strange daughter who had blossomed that evening into such unexpected beauty.

But the rectory was reached and the maids summoned, and all except Frederica, who retired to her room, ran about getting the bedchambers prepared.

Frederica sat by the window, her heart beating hard, wondering if it had all been a dream. She scarcely could take in that she would marry Rupert and spend the rest of her days with him, bear his children.

Amy's petulant voice sounded along the corridor: "Is Frederica already too grand to help us?"

Frederica jolted herself out of her reverie and went to carry clean sheets to the little-used bedchambers. "And to think," said her mother, "the number of times I have bemoaned that the rectory was too large for us. Dr. Hadley has the right of it. The Crowns can be as insulting as they like. We need not care about them any longer."

"I wonder what they will do?" mused Frederica. "They are so very grand and proud. I do not think they will be able to stay away. If I am not mistaken, they will be rallying already and trying to persuade the guests that they knew of Lord Granton's intentions toward me all along."

"But how did you meet him?" demanded Mary, fussily arranging flowers beside the bed in which Lord Granton was to sleep. "He cannot have fallen in love with you simply after a few visits to the rectory where you were abominably rude to him."

"We used to meet in the evenings and walk and talk," said Frederica dreamily.

"But what was he about?" asked Mary. "Had he not proposed and had you been seen together, it would have been a great scandal, and no one would have wanted to marry you."

"You had all led me to believe that no one would want to marry me anyway," pointed out Frederica. "At first we were friends, that was all, and he taught me to dance."

Mrs. Hadley looked at Frederica in horror. "You took a dangerous risk. Did you not think of his reputation?"

"There was nothing in his behavior to frighten or shock me. He looked on me as an amusing little girl, until . . ." Frederica broke off and smiled.

"Until?" prompted Amy eagerly.

But Frederica felt her mother would be far too shocked if she told them that it was until he had kissed her in the church, a kiss that she had begged for.

There was a rumble of carriage wheels outside. "They are come!" cried Mrs. Hadley.

As they stepped down from the carriage, Lord Granton drew the major aside. "Did I hear you right? You said Annabelle told you she would marry you after all and you refused her?"

"What would you?" said the major sadly. "She was burning up with humiliation and any man would do. I do not want her on those terms."

"I should think if you had any pride, my friend, you would not want her on any terms."

"I proposed to her twice," said the major. "Twice! And twice she refused me."

"You are too fine a fellow for her."

The major wearily shook his head.

"Ah, here is our host," said Lord Granton as the rector came out to meet them. "We must now cope with the inane chattering of my beloved's sisters."

"Welcome, welcome!" cried Dr. Hadley. "I beg you to join us for supper. Nothing as grand as you would get at the Hall, for we were not expecting to dine here tonight."

Leaving the maids and Gustave to carry in their luggage, Lord Granton and the major followed Dr. Hadley into the drawing room.

He went immediately to sit next to Frederica while her three sisters, silent for once, gazed on them in awe.

Dr. Hadley produced two bottles of champagne and beamed all around. "I had been saving these for a special occasion. We will drink a toast to the happy couple."

The major sat down on the sofa between Amy and Harriet. "I hope I am not crushing you, ladies," he said, indicating his girth. "I am a trifle large."

Amy giggled and flirted with her eyes over her fan. "Was I not saying, t'other day, Harriet, that Major Delisle was a fine figure of a man?"

"Oo, yes," said Harriet. "Very fine."

The major gave a sad little laugh. "I am not much of a ladies' man."

"And all the better for that," declared Amy. "I do despise gentlemen who are so practiced in flirting that one is never able to believe a word they say."

They all drank champagne and then moved through to the dining room to eat "a simple spread," which consisted of the best of cold meats from the larder.

Amy, Harriet, and Mary were competing fiercely for the major's attention, and Lord Granton no longer thought they were silly, tiresome girls as he saw his friend blossom under all the attention.

He murmured to Frederica under the cover of the babble, "Are we never going to be alone? We have so much to talk about."

"The pool," whispered Frederica, "after they have all gone to bed."

"I could come to your room."

"That would never do. One hears everything in this old house. It is only a wonder that I did not learn that I was not invited to the ball."

"What! And yet you came."

"The gracious Lady Crown changed her mind only today and relented. I did not want to go, for the lateness of the invitation was a great insult, but Papa was frightened I would offend them."

"My love, we do not need to run off to the woods any more. I will wait half an hour until everyone has retired and we can walk in the garden. We are a respectable couple now."

But Frederica thought that night that no one was going to retire. Back in the drawing room after dinner, Amy, Harriet, and Mary tried to fascinate the major. Mrs. Hadley sat in a happy dream, and Dr. Hadley asked anxiously when the announcement would appear in the newspapers and, being told by his future son-in-law that it would appear as soon as possible, relapsed into the same happy state as his wife.

At last Frederica pointedly yawned and said she was too tired to stay awake any longer and the party broke up.

Then Frederica had to firmly shoo her sisters out of her bedchamber, her sisters who were avid to hear how she had walked and talked with Lord Granton. When they had gone, she took off her ball gown and laid it tenderly away in its tissue-paper wrappings. She put on her old blue muslin gown and wrapped a brightly colored shawl about her shoulders and went down the back stairs to the garden.

He was pacing up and down, waiting for her, a tall figure in the moonlight. She stopped short, suddenly shy of him.

But he turned and saw her and held out his arms. She ran into them, feeling them close about her, feeling that demanding mouth descending on her own and then feeling nothing but hot, searing passion while the moon, the stars, and the garden whirled about them until there seemed to be only the two of them fused together at the center of a spinning world.

It was when his hand cradled her breast that Mrs. Hadley, who had been watching from the window, felt things had gone far enough.

"Lord Granton!"

Lord Granton reluctantly freed Frederica. "We have been discovered at last," he said with a shaky laugh.

Upstairs, Mrs. Hadley turned to her husband, who was lying in bed. "You had best talk to my lord about getting a special license. I tell you this. Frederica is as much of a problem as she ever was! So abandoned! I could hardly believe my eyes!"

The Crown family held a council of war the following afternoon. Lady Crown had done as much as she could to repair the damage done to Annabelle, saying that Annabelle had been party to the betrothal and had only playacted that scene. But it was evident no one had believed her.

"He is wicked, evil!" cried Sir Giles, pacing up and down. "Do you know what I think? I think he was not writing a book at all but sneaking out like a thief in the night to meet that wretched, scheming little slut from the rectory."

"That Frederica is a witch," said Lady Crown coldly. "Undistinguished, no manners, no breeding. A snake! A viper! And after all we have done for that family. You must tell Dr. Hadley to get out, and as soon as possible."

Annabelle's eyes gleamed. "And I would like to be present when you tell him."

"And so you may," said her father. "I will send a footman to the rectory and have him brought here."

But they waited and waited until the footman returned with a letter. Sir Giles opened it and his face became mottled with rage. "Can you believe this? Dr. Hadley takes leave to inform us that he is unable to call on us because he is engaged in entertaining his guests."

"Then we will go and tell him," hissed Annabelle. "We will tell him to quit the rectory in front of Lord Granton and that dreadful family."

"Wait!" Lady Crown held up one beringed hand for silence. "We are not thinking clearly."

"What is there to think about?" demanded Annabelle. "They must be shamed; they must be humiliated. . . ."

"No," said Lady Crown in a flat voice, "we must not offend them."

"What is this?" Sir Giles looked on the point of having an apoplexy. "Not offend them?"

Lady Crown, who had been pacing, sat down as if suddenly weary. She leaned her head on her hand and said, "Annabelle is not yet wed. She will need another Season next year. Lord Granton is a leader of society, Frederica will be" — she choked a little — "will be his viscountess. If we offend them and they cut us, then what of poor Annabelle's chances? It's not as if anyone wanted her last Season."

"Mama!" Annabelle began to cry, but her mother looked at her coldly. "It is all your fault, Annabelle. You should not have been so blind. You should have tried harder to attract him. Had he fallen for a beauty, our shame would not be so great. But Frederica Hadley of all people! Everyone in London will get to hear of it. Let me think, let me think. There is nothing else to be done. We will need to go to the rectory and congratulate the slut, the jade, with every sign of joy and complacency."

"I would rather die," said Annabelle tearfully.

"You will be dead socially if we do not," rasped Lady Crown.

"Mama!" cried Harriet, who had been looking out of the window of the rectory drawing room. "The Crowns are arrived."

"Come away from the window!" shrieked her mother. "We will say we are not at home. Where is Frederica?"

"Out walking with Lord Granton. Oh dear, too late. Mary has gone to meet them."

Harriet and the major made for the door to escape but found they were met by the Crowns, who were just entering. Lady Crown swanned toward Mrs. Hadley, "We are come to offer our felicitations to your daughter."

"Frederica?"

"Who else?" said Lady Crown with a laugh like brittle glass. "Where is the dear child?"

"Frederica is out walking with Lord Granton."

"Then we must wait for her return." Lady Crown sat down on the sofa and patted the seat next to her to indicate that Annabelle should sit down as well.

The major looked miserably at Annabelle, who

looked miserably back. Her eyes were red and swollen.

He cleared his throat. "Perhaps Miss Annabelle would care to take a walk in the gardens with me?"

"You are too kind." Lady Crown smiled her permission. "Poor Annabelle is still overset by her near escape from death."

"We will go, too," said Amy.

"I am sure that will not be necessary," said Lady Crown with all her old autocratic air. "Annabelle and Major Delisle are already good friends."

The major held out his arm. Annabelle rose and with bowed head and averted eyes walked out with him.

When they were well clear of the house, the major said in a low and sympathetic voice, "I did try to warn you."

"So you did," mumbled Annabelle, "and I treated you shamefully." She looked up at him, her eyes brimming with tears. "Can you ever forgive me?"

"Of course," said the gallant major.

"I was led astray by my parents' ambitions," said Annabelle, whose ambitions had equalled those of her parents but was not going to betray that to this, she now regarded, as her last hope of marriage.

"We will forget about everything and start afresh," said the major. "Did I ever tell you about a vastly amusing play I saw in London?"

Annabelle knew that the major had probably told her already in boring detail about every play he had ever seen in London, but she said, "No, do tell me, sir."

The major talked away busily, laughing at all the remembered comical scenes while Annabelle leaned on his arm and laughed as well, that tinkling laugh taught to young ladies by singing masters that started at the top of the scale and ran down it.

They did not even notice Lord Granton and Frederica returning from their walk and entering the rectory.

Mrs. Hadley had been dreading this encounter between Frederica and Lady Crown. Looking up as her daughter entered the room, she stifled a groan, for Frederica's lips were swollen and her hair was in disarray. She carried her bonnet in her hand.

Frederica stopped short at the sight of Lady Crown and Sir Giles.

Lady Crown rose to her feet. "We are come to offer you our felicitations, my dear, and apologize for any unpleasantness, and to you, too, Lord Granton. I am afraid we had the silly idea that you were to propose to Annabelle, but now I see how stupid we have been."

"We accept your apology," said Lord Granton, giving Frederica's hand a warning press.

"Yes, indeed," said Frederica coldly. "I beg you to excuse me. I am hot from walking and must change."

"Ah, but my little Annabelle is anxious to apologize to you as well. Here is the dear girl."

Annabelle came in on the arm of Major Delisle, looking radiant. "Major Delisle and I are to be wed, Mama!" she cried. "Papa, give us your blessing."

But Frederica murmured a hurried excuse and fled from the room. Lady Crown's glare at her daughter spoke volumes. Frederica was to be a viscountess while her own daughter was going to be only the wife of a soldier.

Frederica and Lord Granton were married three months later in the village church. The splendor of her jewels and of her wedding gown was talked of by the villagers for years to come.

Lady Crown had offered the hall for the wedding breakfast, but Frederica and Lord Granton said it would be held in the rectory.

Lady Crown felt bitterly that it was really so like the Hadleys to invite the whole village so that one found oneself rubbing shoulders with people like the butcher and the baker.

Annabelle was not present. She had sent her excuses to say that she was feeling unwell. She was bitterly regretting her decision to wed a mere major and did not want to watch Frederica marrying a lord. Annabelle was on the point of begging her parents to find a way of releasing her from the engagement. She was soon to go to London, a London full of earls, marquesses, and dukes, and she wanted to go unencumbered by Major Delisle.

She did not know that the major, standing in front of the altar by his friend Lord Granton, was paying little attention to the wedding service. Instead he was wondering how to escape from Annabelle Crown, whom he had begun to find every bit as tedious and boring as his friend once had.

Lady Crown thought sourly that Frederica did not look virginal at all. Instead she looked indecently happy.

She was in the hall of the rectory after the wedding breakfast as Frederica was about to mount the stairs to change into her traveling clothes, for Frederica and her new husband were to start their married life at his house in London before moving to his place in the country. "I wish you well, my dear," Lady Crown said, her eyes narrowing. "But I confess I never took you for a sophisticate."

Frederica paused, one hand on the newel post, the other holding up the white lace train of her wedding gown. "What does that mean?" she demanded.

"I assume you know that once a rake, always a rake. But before your husband goes philandering again, I advise you to make sure to produce an heir."

Frederica turned and marched up the stairs, her head high.

But Lady Crown's words began to burn and

sear. How could she expect Rupert to remain faithful to her?

"You are very silent, my love," said Lord Granton at last when they were in the carriage alone together and had waved good-bye to the guests.

"I am wondering what I will do when you are unfaithful to me."

"Why on earth should I be unfaithful to you?"

"Because you are a rake."

He held her close. "I am a rake who has fallen in love for the first time and the last. Now kiss me and do not talk any more fustian."

Lord Granton was to marvel later how all his dreams of tenderly making love properly to his wife for the first time in a goose-feather bed had come to nothing as he and Frederica, gasping and clawing and kissing and panting, fell onto the carriage floor.

But Frederica had never behaved like any woman he had ever met.

And she probably never would!

The employees of G.K. Hall hope you have enjoyed this Large Print book. All our Large Print titles are designed for easy reading, and all our books are made to last. Other G.K. Hall books are available at your library, through selected bookstores, or directly from us.

For information about titles, please call:

(800) 257-5157

To share your comments, please write:

Publisher
G.K. Hall & Co.
P.O. Box 159
Thorndike, ME 04986